Be a Writing Superstar

by
Joel A. Sutherland

Illustrated by
Patricia Storms

Scholastic Canada Ltd.
Toronto New York London Auckland Sydney
Mexico City New Delhi Hong Kong Buenos Aires

Scholastic Canada Ltd.
604 King Street West, Toronto, Ontario M5V 1E1, Canada

Scholastic Inc.
557 Broadway, New York, NY 10012, USA

Scholastic Australia Pty Limited
PO Box 579, Gosford, NSW 2250, Australia

Scholastic New Zealand Limited
Private Bag 94407, Botany, Manukau 2163, New Zealand

Scholastic   Children's Books
Euston House, 24 Eversholt Street, London NW1 1DB, UK

Library and Archives Canada Cataloguing in Publication
Sutherland, Joel A., 1980-
   Be a writing superstar / Joel A. Sutherland ; illustrated by Patricia Storms.
ISBN 978-0-545-98000-5
   1. Authorship--Juvenile literature. 2. Creative writing--Juvenile
literature. I. Storms, Patricia II. Title.
PN159.S88 2010   j808'.02   C2010-901825-7

6 5 4 3 2 1   Printed in Canada 121   10 11 12 13 14

Table of Contents

Acknowledgements

Early Tip 1

After you've written your first book, don't forget to thank all the people who have directly or indirectly helped you through the process. Otherwise, your parents might stop buying you birthday presents, your siblings might not let you borrow their coolest stuff anymore and your friends might put your hand in a bowl of warm water at the next sleepover.

I'd like to thank my friends and family, each and every one. Please don't make me pee in my sleeping bag.

Thanks to everyone at the Ajax Public Library (where I began writing silly interviews for the library's newsletter), for your support and encouragement over the last six years.

I wouldn't be where I am today without the mentorship of both Ken Setterington and Peter Carver, two of the biggest forces in Canadian children's publishing — and two of the nicest teachers/mentors I've ever had.

An extra-special thank you is much deserved for the incredible crew at Scholastic who had a hand in this book's creation. This includes (but isn't limited to) Diane Kerner, Patricia Storms, Andrea Casault, Maureen Johnson and Jennifer MacKinnon, an editor extraordinaire who has had to put up with me without once calling me a moron, contrary to my claim later in this book (consider that a piece of creative non-fiction). This book is equally yours as it is mine.

Dedication

Early Tip 2

A dedication lists to whom you would like to dedicate the book (obviously!). Unlike the acknowledgements, it's rare to dedicate a book to all of your friends and family, as well as your editor. Instead, dedications are for one or two individuals. Say you won a new television, and you decided to give it away as a gift. Would you divide it into twenty-five equal pieces and give one piece to each of your classmates, or would you give it — fully intact and watchable — to one special person?

I'd like to dedicate this book — the whole TV — to my best friend and wife, Colleen Morris. Not only did you show impeccable taste when you married me (ahem), but you made me the happiest guy in the world.

Look at that — we haven't even got to the introduction yet and you've already picked up a couple of valuable tips!

Introduction for Kids

No Adults Allowed That Means You Mom!

Writing is fun.

No, seriously. It is. Really, really fun.

Okay, well, some kinds of writing are a little less fun than others. Writing a grocery list? Not so much fun, and it always makes me hungry. Writing a geography test? Not so much fun, and it always makes me Hungary (must be all the Turkey).

Writing a story about magic-duelling wizards, crime-fighting superheroes, famous-landmark-exploding aliens, bloodsucking (and super-cute) vampires or lovey-dovey heartthrobs? Now that's fun!

The book you're holding in your hands — I'm referring to *Be a Writing Superstar* (which should be obvious, unless you have the ability to read two books at once and have one in each hand) — is the perfect book for you. I don't even know you, but I know that this is the perfect book for you. You know how I know? Because this is the perfect book for kids of all ages and writing-skill levels. Whether you're a JK student dreaming of becoming the next J.K. Rowling or someone who shudders when teachers hand out creative writing assignments, this book will prove that writing is fun.

Speaking of fun, you might have noticed from the Table of Contents (if you're a Table of Contents-reading kind of person) that this book is jam-packed with cool stuff you normally wouldn't find in books on writing. And if you're not a Table of Contents-reading kind of person and have no idea what I'm blabbering on about, here's a promise from me to you:

2

I, Joel A. Sutherland, author of *Be a Writing Superstar*, do solemnly swear that the book you're holding in your hands (you know the one, unless you're still reading two books at once, in which case I'm starting to think you're a little weird) will not contain any boring bits. It is not a textbook. It is not an instructional manual. It is not a grammar guide.

It is a book of fun and games. Of silly interviews. Of arts and crafts and party planning tips. Of moose poo.

I also solemnly swear to floss every day. Cavities are the pits, and I'm a little afraid of my dentist.

Joel A. Sutherland

Everyone has the ability to write a great story, and the proof is in this book. With nothing more than a pencil, a sheet of paper and a library card, you'll have your eyes opened to a world of wordy wonder. You'll be taught the Nuts and Bolts of the writing craft, from brainstorming ideas straight through to hosting your own book launch for friends and family. You'll trade laughs and bons mots with your pals as you get your literary Game On. You'll be reminded of the oldest cliché in the book (pardon the pun): that to be a writer you have to be a reader, so Don't Forget to Read (Duh!).

Last but not least, you'll be treated to **5 Silly Questions** with some of your favourite authors and illustrators. These interviews are a hilarious reminder that writers are funny people and writing is, above all else, fun.

So without any further ado, put your hands together for our first silly interviewee, Robert Munsch!

Wait!
Hold your applause! We have one more formality — the introduction for adults. Sheesh!

Introduction
for Adults

Mom Wuz Here!

Hey, adults! Welcome to your very own introduction. Are you excited? I know I am!

You didn't read the "Introduction for Kids," did you?

No?

You promise?

Good.

Let me tell you how to use this book to encourage your kids (children, students and young library customers alike) to write. I'll make this snappy since I heard a bit of applause a moment ago and Robert Munsch is starting to grow a tad impatient.

First, I should note that while most of the silly interviews were recently written for this book, some were written over the last few years for my library's newsletter. Although some of the questions reflect this, I believe that the interviews remain fun little vignettes into the authors' lives and will be inspirational for your children and students who have been bitten by the writing bug — or those you wish to *have* bitten!

Second . . .

Wait a minute, are you sure you didn't read the "Introduction for Kids?"

You did? *How could you?*

What do you mean, you "didn't know you weren't supposed to read it?" It says it clearly right there in the title: "Introduction . . . FOR KIDS."

And they call ME a monster!

Well, I don't think it's fair that you get to read *two* introductions. Not fair at all. I have no other option but to cancel this introduction. It's tough, but fair.

You're just going to have to figure everything out on your own as we go along.

And stop crying, Dad. If you do the crime, be prepared to do the time. Oh, for heaven's sake. Will someone get him a tissue?

You're ready for Mr. Munsch now? That was faster than scheduled! What ever happened to professionalism?

5 Silly Questions
with Robert Munsch

JS: Wow, I'm a little star-struck; you're a living legend and I grew up devouring your books. With over 48 picture books, a handful of treasuries, a bucketful of on-line stories and a boatload of poems published to date, you're certainly prolific. I don't really know where to begin, and look at that: I've wasted all the space I had for my first question without asking a question. Sorry.

RM: This is "star stuck," not "star struck."

JS: Having written so many books, you must be starting to run out of titles. Any regrets that you used up two titles for both *Jonathan Cleaned Up – Then He Heard a Sound or Blackberry Subway Jam* and *Giant or Waiting for the Thursday Boat*?

RM: Yes, lots of regrets. I could have had two more books if I had saved those titles.

JS: I once saw Joey on the sitcom *Friends* cry when he read *Love You Forever*. Having emptied a box of tissues every time I've read it myself, I know that Joey's not the only one to shed a few tears on its pages. Do you have a secret deal with the Kleenex company?

RM: How did you know about the Kleenex deal? That is top secret! I get one Garbanzian Skwonk for every box of Kleenex that is sold.

JS: I seem to recall that when *I Have To Go!* was originally released it had one more word in the title . . . the word sounded like the letter found between O and Q — it's associated with the number 1 and you wouldn't want to eat snow coloured by it. What happened?

RM: It was originally just called *Pee* and then Annick Press changed it to *Hold Everything* and then Michael Martchenko changed it to *I Have To Go!* I am now working on a book called *100 Fun Things To Do With Moose Poo.*

JS: Many of your books, such as *Thomas' Snowsuit* and *Stephanie's Ponytail*, are named after real kids. Hypothetically, if I sent you $20 in the mail, is there any chance your next book could be *Joel's Big Nose*, and if not, how do I go about getting my hypothetical $20 back?

RM: It costs $1,000,000 to get in a book. Nobody has ever offered me that, so it is just sort of luck that kids get in my books. If you send me $20, I am just going to keep it because you are a cheapo librarian and I found this picture of you on the internet:

Robert Munsch grew up in Pittsburgh, Pennsylvania, and now lives in Guelph, Ontario, although his mother says he never grew up and still acts like he's six years old. Robert insists that he acts like a very mature six-year-old. His books have earned him many accolades, legions of fans and mountains of Garbanzian Skwonks.

Nuts and Bolts

It Was a Dark and Stormy Night . . . In Your Brain!

Now that it's time to get down to it, let's begin at the beginning, shall we? Seems a reasonable thing to do.

Picture this: lightning strikes. Thunder booms. Rain pours. Wind howls. Cats and dogs claw and nip at each other as they plummet from the sky. People run about with folded newspapers held above their heads, cursing their stupidity for not bringing an umbrella, even though the weatherman warned of showers. (But when is the weatherman ever right?)

Now picture this pandemonium happening *inside your head!*

It's called brainstorming, but don't worry, you don't need to wear rubber boots to do it. Brainstorming is the act of freeing your imagination to think of as many story ideas as you can while your hand records these ideas on a piece of paper. It's a great place to start before you begin writing, whether you already have a great story idea or have no idea what to write about at all. Ideas, after all, don't grow on trees. People often ask me,

Where do you get your ideas?

Joel A. Sutherland's ravenous fans

Walmart

Joel A. Sutherland

But that's not really true: Walmart's selection of ideas is sadly lacking these days, so I brainstorm. Here's how you can, too!

What you need:

- ✔ Your imagination (pretty much a necessity at every stage of writing).

- ✔ A quiet, comfortable room, or the superhuman ability to block out the crying baby seated next to you on the bus.

- ✔ Pen/pencil/marker/crayon/lump of coal.

- ✔ Paper (writing on the walls is not a good idea — just ask the four-year-old me, or my mother).

- ✔ A stopwatch. Yes, a stopwatch. Okay, a regular old watch will work, too. What do you need a stopwatch for? Hold on — you'll see soon!

How to do it:

1. Get comfy in your quiet room, or block out the crying baby on the bus.

2. Decide on a reasonable amount of time to brainstorm. Five to seven minutes is usually sufficient. Set a stopwatch (see?), or jot the end time down on the top of your paper as a reminder.

3. Write a topic for your story in the centre of the paper and circle it. This can be very short ("vampires") or a little more detailed ("female high school student falls for male vampire"). It can even be a quick drawing, like mine:

4. Clear your mind. This is easier for some people than others. For me, it's remarkably easy. For a smart cookie like you, it's probably staggeringly difficult. Sit back, close your eyes, take a few deep breaths and feel all your cares and concerns and crying babies slip away.

5. Now, here's the fun part. Pick up your pen and write down anything that comes to mind. Draw lines and circles to connect related ideas. Do this as quickly as possible, using abbreviations and shorthand, and whatever you do don't stop to think about what you've jotted down — in fact, don't think at all! Just write, write, write.

6. Once the time or your ideas run out, you're all done. Take a look at what you've written. It won't all be perfection (or even make sense), but I guarantee you'll find something in your brainstorming that will spark your creative lightning!

Now, while you enjoy a silly interview with Adrienne Kress, I'll be writing a best-selling novel about a water-skiing, Canadian Idol-watching, giraffe-loving vampire and the girl who falls for him despite the fact that he's, um, a water-skiing, Canadian Idol-watching, giraffe-loving vampire.

5 Silly Questions
with Adrienne Kress

JS: I was expecting the titular gentleman in *Alex and the Ironic Gentleman* to be a gentleman who is not gentle at all, but rather mean-spirited, ill-tempered and unopposed to public flatulence . . . the complete opposite of a true gentleman. But the *Ironic Gentleman* turned out to be a pirate ship! And Alex is a girl often mistaken for a boy due to her haircut and name. Some might call this a stretch of epic, yoga-like proportions on my part, but I'm sensing a connection: is mistaken identity a recurring theme in your writing?

AK: No. But false conclusions are a theme in my writing. It's a personal pet peeve of mine, and something I find humans do with great frequency. They project their own personal views onto a pragmatic situation, and come out with wild conclusions that have no foundation. Like thinking I am interested in mistaken identity. So, yes, I like to play around with that.

JS: The German title of *Alex and the Ironic Gentleman* is *Die halsüberkopfundkragendramatischabenteuerliche Katastrophenexpedition der Alex Morningside*. How does one say this title aloud without either fainting or needing a pee break?

AK: You don't. Invariably both happen. Which is why I would recommend going to the washroom first.

JS: The villain in *Timothy and the Dragon's Gate* is called the Man in the Beige Linen Suit. While he's waiting for his beige linen suit to be returned from the dry cleaner on laundry day, is he temporarily addressed as the Man in Hole-y Sweat Pants and an Old Mustard-Stained T-Shirt?

AK: Actually you will note I took care of that in the novel by pointing out he has several beige linen suits. He's kind of like me. When I go shopping and find something that actually fits I buy many versions of it. It's quite practical. But I will admit that when people refer to you by what you are wearing, it is pretty hard to live up to all the time. I imagine when he does on the odd occasion wear the hole-y sweat pants and mustard-stained T-shirt, he does it where no one can see. I mean, come on, imagine the scandal if he was caught.

JS: You began your writing career, before the publication of your first two novels, as a playwright. I'm famed from coast to coast for my unparalleled use of puns, but don't worry, I'm not going to throw any lame ones at you, like "playwrong" or "playleft." I was actually wondering if you ever had any temptation to label yourself as a novel wrighter?

AK: No. No I haven't. Don't be silly. However, I have had the temptation to call myself "The Fantabulous Creator Of Wonder and Glory With Shiny Hair Who Is Revered Throughout the Land."

JS: *The New York Post* labelled you as one of the six authors to fill the void left by J.K. Rowling. Congrats on the high praise! But what happens if you're the victorious void-filler, and then Ms Rowling decides she wants her void back?

AK: We fight to the death. Or hug and decide to share.

Adrienne Kress is a writer, actor and director born and raised in Toronto, Ontario. Although not a novel wrighter, she is a Fantabulous Creator. As the daughter of two high school English teachers, it is little wonder that she fell in love with both creating and performing the written word.

Game On

I Mistakenly Mistook That Mistake for the Real Thing

I love games. Games of all varieties: card, board, video. Athletic games, mind games, silly games. It doesn't matter. I love games.

Writing games are some of the best games. As you play them, you're not only having fun, but you're warming up your creative juices at the same time. It's like hitting two birds with one stone.

> I hate that expression! How about, It's like hitting two humans with one poop!

One of my favourite writing games is Silly Story Shout-Out. All you need is a silly story and a bunch of people who like to shout. I'll supply the first silly story, but you've got to find the shouters. The story can be about anything, but it works best if it's somewhat realistic. Fantasy, sci-fi and horror won't work very well for this particular game. My apologies to the water-skiing vampires of the world.

However, spread throughout this realistic story are a handful of "sillies" — things that are wrong, don't make a heckuva lot of sense or are just plain stupid.

The rules are simple:

1. One person reads the silly story aloud.

2. Everyone else listens.

3. Whenever one of the sillies pops up in the story, the listeners throw their hands in the air.

4. The reader points to the person who raised his or her hand first, and that person shouts out the silly.

5. If they were right, they get one point. If they were wrong, they lose one point and the next person gets a chance to answer. And if anyone cheats by raising their hand long before a silly is read and keeping it up (knowing that a silly is likely just around the corner — there's one in every crowd), they lose two points.

6. The person with the most points at the end of the story wins!

Here's a short story I whipped up that you could use. The "sillies" are underlined (and yes, the title is underlined, but no, it doesn't count as a "silly," although yes, it is a silly title).

17

Sniff the Dog

By Joel A. Sutherland

Maya was watching TV when her mother told her to take the dog, Sniff, for a walk. So she turned off the TV, picked up the leash and put it on her <u>cat</u>.

It was a very hot day, and after walking for five minutes, Sniff was thirsty. So Maya walked to the stream where Sniff had a drink of <u>root beer</u>.

Once Sniff was feeling refreshed, they went to the park. They played fetch with a <u>rope</u> and tug-of-war with a <u>ball</u>.

Sniff liked stopping at every tree along the way to, er, do his doggie duty. Maya told him the names of the trees as he, er, lightened the load: maple, pine, birch and <u>carrot</u>.

Then it was lunchtime. They were both starving so they decided to <u>not</u> eat their food.

After lunch Maya decided to read Sniff a story. The dog curled up in her lap as Maya <u>sang</u> the book to him.

Now that he had eaten, played some games and had heard a story, Sniff was feeling very sleepy. He had a big yawn, ate a grasshopper and promptly fell asleep. Maya did the same, except for the grasshopper-eating bit. They slept for an hour, and when they woke up the sun was just starting to <u>rise</u>.

It was now late and time to go home. They waved to all their neighbours as they passed by and then they were at their door. Sniff turned to the girl and said, "That was a fun day, <u>Susie</u>. You're my best friend."

THE END

Hey, dogs can't speak! Unless they're wearing special collars of the Disney-animated-movie variety . . . but still, let's count that as a "silly," shall we?

Now that you've used my story (and loved every minute of it, I'm sure), it's time to write one or two of your own. You can have your friends and family write a few, too. It couldn't be easier to do, so let's start one together. Any real life, day-to-day setup will work. How about getting ready for school?

Getting Ready for School

By Joel A. Sutherland and Me

The buzzing of my alarm clock was followed by the screeching of my mother's vocal cords.

"GET UP!" she yelled. "YOU'RE GOING TO BE LATE FOR SCHOOL!"

I tumbled out of bed and stumbled over to my clothes dresser. I put on a T-shirt, a pair of socks, jeans and, last of all, my underwear. I walked downstairs and enjoyed a bowl of bran cereal that my mother had ready for me.

Did you spot the silly? Of course you did! *Nobody* enjoys bran cereal!

I do!

Now keep writing the story, occasionally adding sillies as you go. The easiest way to do this is to write a normal story, and then go back and switch some actions, objects or people with silly stuff.

For example, switch this:

I walked up the steps and said good morning to the man driving the bus.

To this:

I walked up the steps and said good morning to the octopus driving the bus.

If your friends don't catch this silly, I suggest you find some new friends.

5 Silly Questions
with Seán Cullen

JS: While talking about *Hamish X and the Hollow Mountain,* you've said, "I've already read it . . . because I wrote it . . . and I read it while I wrote it. That's how these things work." I never knew that! What other trade secrets can you share with us about the workings of writing?

SC: One thing that people overlook when writing a book is that one must be able to read as well. How many great novels have been lost because the author merely wrote "squiggle squiggle squiggle: squiggle squiggle squiggle squiggle squiggle. Squiggle squiggle squiggle squiggle squiggle squiggle squiggle squiggle squiggle squiggle squiggle squiggle. Squiggle squiggle squiggle, squiggle squiggle!" Good punctuation but little in the way of story.

JS: The first book in your latest fantasy series is about a prince of "neither here nor there." How does one become a prince of neither here nor there, exactly? Are you elected by neither citizens nor countrymen, or born by either a royal papa or a monarch mama who happen to be neither king nor queen?

SC: First of all, one must be born of noble parents who have status neither here nor there. Then there is an elaborate vetting process where a panel of judges decides to accept or not accept your petition. Next, once they have made neither decision you must be accepted in an extensive voting process involving balloting by people who are registered citizens of neither Here Nor There. If that goes as planned or not planned, you are chosen as a Prince of Neither Here Nor There. Simple really.

JS: There's a rousing pirate shanty that plays on the Hamish X website about Cheesebeard the Pirate King, sung by a man with a voice only a pirate's mother could love. Which, as it turns out, is exactly what it takes to sing a good pirate shanty. But tell me, what does this man look like? (I like to picture him with only one of many body parts: one eye, one hand, one leg, one nipple and so on and so forth.)

SC: The singer is Febster Bellwagon, a famous shanty singer. He sings in shanties across the globe to dishevelled audiences. He is missing the centre of his chest, one leg, the bones of his right arm and has a moustache made out of creamed corn. He is putting out an album very soon entitled "My Mother Happens to Love My Voice!" Watch for it.

JS: Before you wrote fantasy novels, you wrote a lot of your own material as a successful stand-up comedian. How do the two processes differ?

SC: Writing stand-up comedy material is very different from writing a novel. First of all, it's shorter. And you don't have to worry about spelling because you are talking instead of writing it down. Also, while writing a novel, no one starts shouting at you to be funnier or to shut up. However, I often shout insults at books, but I think I'm a little unusual.

JS: If Hamish X could travel to any exotic location in the world (for the sake of argument, let's pretend he has a sister who happens to be a stewardess, entreating him to discounted airfare and all the tiny packages of peanuts he can eat), would he still go to Providence, Rhode Island?

SC: Hamish X is irresistibly drawn to a confrontation with the Grey Agents in their headquarters at Providence, Rhode Island. If he were free to go anywhere, however, he would very much like to go to the jungles of Borneo to search for the mysterious Flooring Ape, a primate whose call is eerily similar to a human voice shouting "FLOOOOOOOOOOOOOOOOOOOORING!" Its mysterious call brings floor-covering enthusiasts from all over the world, eager to catch a glimpse of this rare beast.

Seán Cullen is one of the busiest people in the world. Not only is he an author and comedian, but he also regularly performs for stage, screen and radio, and it is rumoured that he moonlights as Febster Bellwagon, the famous shanty singer.

Write Like a Wizard

You passed. Is this thing on?

Chances are you're a muggle. And if you're a muggle like me, you love fantasy stories. If magic, wizards, witches and dragons stir your cauldron, here are some tips to help you write your own fantasy:

1. Fantasies come in all shapes and sizes: short stories, novellas and super-sized epics. How long is your story going to be? To avoid becoming overwhelmed, you might want to start out small, but if the story begins to balloon into a behemoth, go with it.

2. A good writer is always prepared, especially when writing fantasy. Create a timeline for your world's history, draw a map of the terrain and write a list of your characters' physical, emotional and intellectual traits. The more you know about your made-up world and characters, the more real they will seem for the reader.

3. But hey, don't feel like you have to make up everything! Feel free to borrow elements from classic mythology and other fantasies — just make sure to put original twists on them. J.K. Rowling, J.R.R. Tolkien and C.S. Lewis all did this in their fantasy novels.

Tip
Having trouble finding reliable and exciting information about classical mythologies? Might I suggest a trip to your local library?

4. After you've written a first draft, edit your story with an eagle eye. Make sure it is . . .

   - consistent. All fantasies, although not real, have their own set of rules. Once you've established yours, don't break them!
   - populated by likable, realistic characters. Sure, your main character is a ten-metre-tall talking eggplant, but that doesn't mean he should act like a vegetable. Even though your characters might not be human, and the world they live in is complete make-believe, try basing them on people from real life: a good friend, a mean teacher, a handsome and dashing author of a creative writing book with the word "superstar" in the title.
   - filled with enough information to entice a reader, but not so much that it becomes a burden to read. Don't hit us over the head with all the planning you did before writing. Instead, sprinkle it throughout the story.

5. Consider shortening your first name and middle initial(s) to single letters followed by periods. Seems like a popular thing to do among fantasy writers.

Have you read all the adventures that take place in Hogwarts, Middle-earth and Narnia? Here are some further fantasy settings to travel to:

- Watership Down, as seen through the eyes of a group of rabbits, in Richard Adams' *Watership Down*
- Redwall, in Brian Jacques' *Redwall* and its sequels
- The underground world filled with demons, robots and talking animals in Kazu Kibuishi's graphic novel series, Amulet
- The Lower Elements in Eoin Colfer's Artemis Fowl books
- Camp Half-Blood in Rick Riordan's *Percy Jackson and the Olympians: The Lightning Thief*
- Tree Haven, Hibernaculum and Underworld, in Kenneth Oppel's Silverwing Saga

Speaking of Kenneth Oppel, let's bring him out for an interview!

5 Silly Questions
with Kenneth Oppel

JS: What has better odds: writing a book in high school, sending it to author Roald Dahl, who passes it on to his agent, who then gets it published (as happened with your first book, *Colin's Fantastic Video Adventure*); or, winning the lottery, being struck by lightning and shooting a hole in one, all simultaneously?

KO: Teen prodigies are a dime a dozen now. Look at Gordon Korman and Chrisopher Paolini and Nancy Yi Fan. Anyone who's anyone is publishing before 18 these days. I blame video games, TV and the Internet.

JS: Your second book was written in your final year at the University of Toronto. Have you at any time in your life focused on your studies instead of your writing?

KO: Ah, well, I wrote that second book as part of my studies. I got a full-year course credit for it. I was very studious in high school, moderately studious in university (I was just as interested in writing for the student newspaper and making awful little student films) and since graduating I've studiously avoided conventional work so I could write full-time.

JS: *Silverwing* and *Sunwing* tell the story of Shade, a runt bat on a dangerous journey, while *Firewing* is about the adventures of Shade's child. The fourth book of the series, *Darkwing*, is set 65 million years in the past and is about the world's first bat, Dusk. Tell me, have you compiled a complete family tree from Dusk to Shade, and if so, if Shade were to meet Dusk, how many times would he need to say "great" before "grandfather?"

KO: The family tree would truly be immense. There would be more "begats" than the Bible.

JS: If you had become a detective instead of an author, which case would you rather investigate (as in the *Barnes and the Brains* series): ghosts, magic, robots, dinosaurs, super-goo or vampires? Why?

KO: I think the more probing investigation would be A Bad Case of Sequels. All I see anywhere are sequels. When will the madness end?

JS: While reading *Airborn* and *Skybreaker*, the geek in me (I've been told that's about 97% of me) thrilled to the imagination and fantasy behind airships, cloud cats, hydrium, flying pirates, aerozoans and lost gold. Can you further thrill my inner geek by giving us a teaser for the third book in the series? Oh, wait, let me back up a bit: will there be a third book in the series?

KO: Of course there will be a third book. I'm working on it right now. It's going to be called *Starclimber*, and it's about the very first journey into outer space — a Canadian expedition it turns out, with both Matt Cruse and Kate de Vries aboard.

Bestselling author Kenneth Oppel lives in Toronto with his family. Starclimber was released in 2008 and was nominated for the Red Maple Award, and I, for one, hope the madness never ends.

Don't Forget to Read (Duh!)

My Books Are Mine, Mine, Mine . . . But We Can Share

Stop me if you've heard this joke before:

A young girl comes home from school and sits down on the couch. Her mother sits next to her and asks, "How was your day at school?"

The girl smiles from ear to ear. "It was great," she says. "Teacher taught us how to write!"

"Oh, that's marvelous," her mother replies, giving the girl a great big hug. "I'm so proud of you — my little baby's growing up. What did you write?"

"I have no idea," the girl says with a shrug of her shoulders. "Teacher hasn't taught us how to read yet."

I don't have to tell you how important reading is, especially if you want to improve your writing. Many successful authors, when asked how to become a published writer, tell people to read, read often and then read some more. Perhaps they're on to something.

Books are magical. They act as vehicles that can whisk you away to far away places or even far away times. They allow you to get inside the heads of people completely different from yourself. They can make you laugh, cheer, cry, chaff, fear, fly. Look at me — I'm making myself all emotional just thinking about books. Give me a moment, please.

Bow down before me, puny humans!

Thank you. I'm better now. My point is, books deserve to be treated as treasured possessions. Here are a few of ways to make sure your books get the respect they deserve:

1. Proudly display your favourite books on your desk, bookshelves or bedside table. Go a little further and arrange your Hogwarts memorabilia around your prized collection of Harry Potter novels. Put a pair of false vampire teeth and a rubber bat next to your books about bloodsuckers. Ask an honest-to-goodness wimpy kid to stand next to your copies of the Diary of a Wimpy Kid books (don't worry about irritating him — he's wimpy).

2. Make your own bookends to help your books stand up straight. Your lazy books will thank you! There are plenty of creative ways to make bookends, such as:

   - Filling jars or bottles with coloured sand, stones or fish tank gravel
   - Painting bricks to look like snowmen, pigs, people, etc.
   - Cutting an old shoebox, as follows:
     - a Recycle the lid and cut-away one of the long panels of the box.
     - b With the cut-away side facing you, use a ruler to draw a line along the middle of the bottom of the box (see illustration).
     - c Using the ruler again, draw a line from the middle of the back panel up to the top left corner.
     - d Use the ruler one more time (Man, is that ever a handy ruler!) to draw a line from the middle of the back panel up to the top right corner.
     - e Cut along all of the lines, creating two halves.

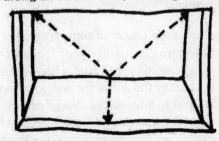

   f And presto bingo banjo — you've got two bookends.

9 But wait — there's more! Decorate your bookends however you like, using markers, crayons, paint, wrapping paper or anything else you can rustle up. Look, I used the comics page from a newspaper. Now I laugh with delight every time I go to select a book to read!

3. Proudly claim ownership of your treasured editions with a bookplate. Copy the sample on the following page, fill in the blanks and glue or tape it to the inside front cover of your books.

You're now the proud owner of some truly special books, but don't forget to share them. Have your friends over for a book swap! Tell everyone to bring a bag of books that they've read and enjoyed. Display the books for everyone to take a look at, and everyone gets to borrow one. Make sure to write a list of who borrowed which book and from whom. After a week or two, host another book swap to return the books and borrow a new one!

This book is mine, mine, mine.

Just so there's no confusion, my name is:

_____

If I were a book critic, I would give it this many stars:

My favourite character is _____.

The best page is _____ because _____

_____

_____

I finished the book on this date: _____.

Aren't I awesome? No need to answer that — I already

know the answer.

5 Silly Questions
with Shane Peacock

JS: In *Monster in the Mountain*, Dylan's parents want to take their son on a peaceful vacation. So they venture deep into BC's Rocky Mountains, home of the Sasquatch. For their next getaway, might I suggest somewhere more run-of-the-mill, like Florida or, say, a nice B&B in Uxbridge?

SP: Listen, I've been to Florida and I can tell you that's one spot that is far too scary for a respectable young Canadian lad like Dylan (George W. Bush's brother used to run the place). And Uxbridge is out of the question as well . . . never have I been in a more terrifying area; there are suburbs sprouting up all over the place.

JS: In *Unusual Heroes* I learned that Jean Chretien was the best street fighter in his town. Who would you pick to win a Royal Rumble between Stephen Harper, Sir John A. Macdonald, Pierre Trudeau and Kim Campbell?

SP: I'd put big bucks on Campbell. Sir John was a brilliant guy but he might just get into the sauce and P.E.T. was far too flighty and would just want to argue anyway. So that leaves Harper and Campbell. Need I say more?

JS: One of your books, *The Great Farini*, is a biography of a man who walked on a tightrope across Niagara Falls with a washtub strapped to his back, pausing in the middle to do his laundry. Besides risking life and limb to make my socks look their whitest, what do I have to do to be appointed The Great Joel?

SP: Well, the Great Farini was wearing the costume of a washer-woman when he did the laundry act; later he dressed up his adopted son as a beautiful female acrobat and "she" became hugely famous, as "Lulu." So, cross-dressing might be where you would have to start.

JS: Having written and co-produced *Team Spirit*, a CTV documentary about hockey, you must be an expert on the sport. So tell me, who's your pick for the Stanley Cup this year: the Argos or the Raptors?

SP: All right, smart guy, I see what you're doing. The Argos and the Raptors are NOT hockey teams! I am indeed a hockey genius, if I may say so myself . . . and I've got my money on the Jays.

JS: I read somewhere that your next project is a series of books about the young Sherlock Holmes. I tried to find some information about this but I'm no, *ahem*, Sherlock Holmes. Can you fill us in?

SP: Sherlock who? Never heard of him . . . my lips are sealed . . . though they may be unsealed in a few months. Keep your ear to the ground . . . Watson.

Shane Peacock is the renowned author of the Dylan Maples adventures, as well as the author of many other books (including The Boy Sherlock Holmes series — Eye of the Crow, Death in the Air, Vanishing Girl, and The Secret Fiend — which I've had a particular fondness for ever since Shane called me "Watson"), scripts, plays and articles. He lives near Cobourg, Ontario.

Nuts and Bolts

Strap a Pair of Nikes on Your Creativity and Get Writing

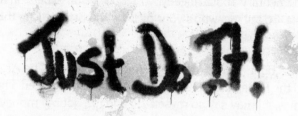

Writer's block, schmiter's schmock.

Dread-filled writers dread the dreaded writer's block. Me? I don't believe it exists. Perhaps that's because I have a Three Step Plan to ensure I'm never beaten by the block (I also have a plan to survive the zombie apocalypse, but that's another book for another day).

The Three Step Plan:

1. Whether one minute or one hour, always set aside some time for writing each and every day. A quiet place may work best, but write wherever, whenever, you like. Write in the morning while you munch on your bran cereal. Write in the afternoon while sitting under a tree at recess. Write at night during the commercial breaks of your favourite singing/dancing/eating-gross-stuff reality show. I've said it before and I'll say it again: write, write, write! (Even during the zombie apocalypse.)

2. Keep your writing area uncluttered and bright. A nice plant can breathe life into your workspace. Keep zombies at a safe distance.

3. Beware of distractions: television, the Internet, your little brother who's lurching towards you with a spaced-out look in his eyes while muttering, "Braaaiiinnnsss." If you've set aside some time to write, don't do anything but.

Still stuck? Don't let the blank page get you down. Here's a Bonus Three Step Plan to overcome writer's block (two plans for the price of one — what value!):

1. Try your hand at free-flow writing. Don't think about what you're writing — just pick up a pen and write without pausing for a second . . . but make sure to stop before you wither away to dust and bones.

2. If you're stuck at the beginning, start with the middle or the end of a story.

3. If all else fails, get up and take a walk. On the outside, this may look like you're breaking the golden rule of doing nothing but writing, but only to a casual observer! What can't be seen is all the brainstorming you'll be doing on the inside as you stroll . . . but don't forget to look where you're going. Nothing ruins a good brainstorm like stepping in a fresh pile of doggie doodle.

There are plenty of ways to kill writer's block (which is lucky, because there are only a couple of ways to kill zombies), so don't be a blockhead!

35

5 Silly Questions
with Andrea and Carolyn Beck

JS: Now that I've got you both here together, I feel I should begin with the question that is at the forefront of your readers' minds, one of great importance to the literary world: growing up together in the Beck household, who was more spoiled?

AB: Carolyn.

CB: Andrea. Well, to tell the truth, we both had a chance to be the "spoiled" kid. I, being the first child, had 2 ½ years of being the only child and Andrea, being the last, was the doted-on baby of the family for at least as long.

AB: Carolyn only thought I was spoiled. Actually, my parents were so worn out from the older two that they relaxed the restrictions by the time I came along, which really ticked her off. Yes!

JS: I've noticed that Andrea's *Elliot Moose* books are split between calm titles *(Elliot Bakes a Cake, Elliot's Bath, Elliot Digs for Treasure, Elliot's Christmas Surprise* and *Elliot's Fire Truck)* and tense titles *(Elliot's Emergency, Elliot's Shipwreck, Elliot's Noisy Night* and *Elliot Gets Stuck).* Carolyn, what does this say about your sister's state of mind?

CB: She could be evenly balanced, evenly unbalanced or a split personality. She's the social worker. Why don't you ask her?

AB: I'm definitely a split personality: writer/illustrator/counsellor. Carolyn's other hat is accounting. She would know about being balanced . . . or unbalanced!

JS: Okay, Andrea, here's your chance to give us the dirt on Carolyn. What kind of an author writes a children's book that necessitates a big stamp on the cover that reads, "WARNING! Do you have the guts to read this book?" as with *The Waiting Dog*?

AB: A twisted one. Given that the art was worse than the words, we used to joke we were the true Twisted Sisters. But back to dirt on Carolyn . . . hmmm . . . yes! She once wrote a story about the caterpillar that pooped out chocolate. Yum! As for childhood, the first bad words she taught me were POO POO PEE PEE KAA KAA. The Sunlight Soap is still lurking in my back molars.

CB: Well . . . in my defense I had to develop guts just to be Andrea's sister.

AB: That is true.

JS: Written by Carolyn and illustrated by Andrea, *The Waiting Dog* gruesomely depicts a dog's fantasy of getting his paws (and teeth) on an unsuspecting postman. Do you think canines also dream of attacking FedEx employees, smoke signalers and/or courier pigeons?

AB: I think they'd rather get dunked in a vat of cheese.

CB: The options are endless — but the story arose from my stint at Hydro Mississauga where I got to hear first-hand tales from the meter readers. Every single one of them had a BITE story. At that time I also had the gentlest, kindest dog in the universe, Brandy, who had a very large voice. She was in the habit of rushing the front door, barking in her deep, deep tones, whenever she heard a rustle outside. But it wasn't to eat the postman or the newsboy or the meter reader; it was all bluff.

I got to thinking . . .

What must those poor people on the other side of our door be thinking? And that was the genesis of *The Waiting Dog*. *The Waiting Dog* is actually told from the perspective of the postman and what he imagines the dog on the other side of the door is imagining. Thank goodness it's all imagination!

JS: It's been a real treat speaking with the both of you. If this interview had a slogan it would have been: "Double your answers, double your tongue twisters / With a silly interview with the Beck sisters." Quick, before the Wrigley's Doublemint Chewing Gum lawyers show up at my door, can you tell us a little about some of your other books?

AB: I'm always thinking of the next Elliot Moose or Pierre Le Poof story. Elliot inhabits a world of friendship and play. He and Socks and the gang tend to get into small scrapes that necessitate teamwork to resolve, as in *Elliot's Fire Truck*. The Elliot stories are gentle, fairly small in scope, such as *Elliot's Bath*, and are meant to create a warm, fun and safe world for younger children. I am currently working on early chapter books for Elliot fans who are moving beyond picture books. Pierre, my darling little poofy poodle, was a refreshing change for me because he has a scampy spark of mischief that gets him into much more trouble than Elliot. His nose for adventure, coupled with his owner's obsession with dog shows, takes him around the big city and out into the world, with trouble at every turn. And Pierre just *looks* ridiculous. Though I am all about story, my books tend to have an underlying theme of kindness, fairness and friendship. I don't write them with that intention, but I guess it's the social worker in me seeping through. I have a couple of novels and screenplays simmering in the background — yikes, too many ideas, not enough time. When my kids move out my writing will explode!

CB: Well, of course there was our other joint venture, *Buttercup's Lovely Day*, which was nominated for the Blue Spruce award. In it a zenfully happy and poetic Holstein named Buttercup (obviously) tells us everything she loves about her life, including the skunk that winds through her legs in the dark. Then there is *Richard Was a Picker*. You can guess what that one's about. *Wellington's Rainy Day* takes us through a day that starts out terribly boring and ends up amazingly satisfying. And *Dog Breath* is an ode to a well-loved pet. Aside from these, I have 100 dog poems in the works, a young adult novel and several more picture books.

Andrea Beck is the author/illustrator of the hit picture book series and TV show Elliot Moose, *and the Pierre Le Poof series of picture books. Educated in Montreal and Toronto, she first made her living as a toy designer then fell in love with the idea of children's stories and art. She currently lives in Unionville, Ontario.*

Carolyn Beck supports her writing habit through freelance accounting work. She now lives in Toronto.

They are rumoured to be debating which one was more spoiled during childhood at this very moment.

Game On

Eat Your Words!

Yum! Writing can be delicious!

Being a food critic must be one of the tastiest jobs I can think of. You get to visit the best restaurants in your city/country/world, eat mouth-watering culinary creations and then write about the meal. Oh, and did I mention people get *paid* to do this? Some people have all the lox.

Like all other avenues of writing, practice makes perfect. In the case of writing food reviews, it can also make you really, really full, so be careful not to overindulge!

Practice being a food critic and grade your favourite restaurants while dining in them. Or better yet, grade your mother's spaghetti tonight (note: the author assumes no responsibility for any groundings that may occur should you give her a negative review). Also, it's not only the food that needs to be critiqued, but these all-important factors as well:

"All the lox?" Seriously? I'm this close to walking out on this gig.

1. The décor: white tablecloths or paper covered in the previous party's tic-tac-toe games?

2. The service: with a smile or with a side of teen angst?

3. The ambiance: soothing music or managers shouting at waiters shouting at cooks shouting at cockroaches skittering across the chicken cordon bleu?

You can even have your friends over to review a three-course meal you'll serve them: gummi leaves for a salad appetizer, gummi worms for the main course and gummi berries for desert. Don't forget gummi pop bottles to wash it all down!

Why not take the idea of eating your words a step further and literally eat some words. Next time your family bakes cookies, forget shaping them in boring old circles. Write some words with the dough instead!

Still hungry? Take a bite out of one of these gastroin-title-nal books:

- *Green Eggs and Ham* by Dr. Seuss
- *Cloudy with a Chance of Meatballs* by Judi Barrett
- *Charlie and the Chocolate Factory* by Roald Dahl
- *Granny Torrelli Makes Soup* by Sharon Creech
- *Crazy for Chocolate* by Frieda Wishinsky
- *Everything on a Waffle* by Polly Horvath
- *How to Eat Fried Worms* by Thomas Rockwell

5 Silly Questions
with Barbara Reid

JS: Your picture books, such as *Perfect Snow*, are illustrated with Plasticine and are incredibly unique. In fact, they're so unique that you and Nick Park, the creator of *Wallace & Gromit*, are two of only a few Plasticine artists in the world. Do you and Nick have an intense Plasticine rivalry? And how many times a day do you say the word Plasticine?

BR: I LOVE *Wallace & Gromit*, and by extension, Nick Park. I like to imagine we would hit it off really well, but so far it is only in my imagination. I don't say Plasticine that often. I'm more likely to say things like, "What should we have for dinner?" and "I haven't seen your socks, where did you have them last?" I've tried having kids say "Plasticine!" instead of "cheese!" for a class photo. It works beautifully if they are on the "cine" part of the word, but if the camera clicks when they are saying "pla" it's not so good.

JS: Your illustrations of animals (*The New Baby Calf, Effie, Have You Seen Birds?*) are remarkably realistic. I've read that many illustrators study animals in the wild to get them right. Do you do this, and if so, how did you find a yeti (*Peg and the Yeti*)?

BR: I've been crazy for animals since I was small, but mostly I draw them from photo reference because real animals won't stay still and they make a mess in the studio. Especially elephants. There aren't many good photos of yetis because most of the climbers on Everest have cold fingers and can't focus the camera very well. Kenneth Oppel's story gave me a sense of the beast, and I filled in the rest with Plasticine (oops, I just said it).

JS: I think it's fantastic how you've incorporated found objects into the illustrations in *The Subway Mouse*. On Nib the mouse's wall there is, among other scraps, a tattered picture of the Cheshire Cat from *Alice in Wonderland*. While I applaud Nib's appreciation of the classics, I'm wondering what kind of a mouse adorns his room with a large-mouthed, sharp-teethed cat?

BR: If you look carefully at the first spread in *The Subway Mouse* you will see a cat in a cage on the subway platform, and near the end of the book there is the terrifying reality of a big orange cat on the prowl. For me *The Subway Mouse* is about the artificial world of the subway, Nib's imaginary world and the real world; maybe those cats represent all three. Don't you sometimes like to scare yourself with imaginary monsters? For the record, Nib and I think the beauty of the real world is worth the risk of the dangers, but I expect we live in the imaginary world a lot of the time. Oh, and I'm as fond of Alice and Lewis Carroll as I am of Wallace, Gromit and Nick. And yes, I ate most of the candy that came in the wrappers that you see in the book, for research, of course.

The orange cat shows up again in *Sing a Song of Mother Goose*, a board book collection of 14 favourite nursery rhymes. She is dressed in Edwardian finery and is frightening a little mouse under the queen's chair. Cats will be cats.

JS: If we threw *Playing with Plasticine* and *Fun with Modeling Clay* into a wrestling ring together, which one would be victorious in having more fun?

BR: It would all be fun until someone got it in the carpet.

JS: The cover of *Fox Walked Alone* shows Fox walking with elephants, lions, green birds, pink flamingoes, polar bears, giraffes, kangaroos and penguins. Well, I suppose the green birds aren't really walking — they're flying — and kangaroos jump while penguins sort of waddle . . . but I'm getting sidetracked. On Planet Barbara, how is the word "alone" defined?

BR: Fox is proud to be an outsider; he just thinks he's alone. It takes most of the book for him to figure out he's not. While Planet Barbara is a very fun place to visit, I feel now and then we all need to be reminded about the rest of the universe. It can't find its socks.

Barbara Reid was born on Planet Barb... er, in Toronto, Ontario, where she currently lives with her husband and two daughters.

Write Like a Superhero

You sure you don't have anything else metallic in your pockets?

It's a bird! It's a plane! It's, well, whatever you want it to be! Instead of Superman, it might be Captain Underpants. Instead of Spider-Man, it might be Magic Pickle. If you were a superhero, what would you be like? Here are some things to consider when writing your own superhero story:

1. Create your superhero.

- Pick a name. It should reflect something about the superhero's personality, strengths or abilities. It shouldn't be too modest (Captain Stronger-Than-Some) or too far-fetched (Mr. Most-Powerful-Being-In-The-Universe-So-You-Might-As-Well-Just-Go-Home-Now-And-Save-Yourself-The-Trouble and his sidekick, Perfect-Hair-And-Straight-Teeth Boy). And don't use an existing name, unless your superhero would rather fight lawsuits than supervillains.

- Pick a superpower. Flight, super strength, super speed, animal/insect abilities — they're good places to start, but why not try to be a little more adventurous? That's easier said than done, especially with the glut of superheroes out there. Take a look at everyday objects and try to think of powers based on them. Among the objects on my desk right now there are a telephone, a pen and computer speakers. I could invent a hero with the ability to talk to anyone in the world without a phone, a hero who can alter reality through his/her creative writing, a hero who can yell loudly enough to topple enemies. Also, there's nothing wrong with using traditional powers, but try to use them in original ways (your hero can fly, except when there's a full moon).

- Pick an alter ego. For every Spider-Man there's a Peter Parker. For every Batman there's a Bruce Wayne. If your hero has to worry about school, work, family matters, a love life and keeping a secret identity — all while trying to save the world — your story will be more relatable to the average reader.

2. Create your supervillain.

- Repeat the first two steps from creating a superhero, but don't worry about all that alter-ego business. Supervillains have the luxury of focusing full-time on their dastardly deeds, all from the comfort of lairs in the bottoms of volcanoes or snow forts in the middle of Antarctica — on account of being insane, and all.

3. Throw in a touch of drama.

- As cool as all the sky-flyin', bad guy-beatin', explosion-dodgin'-in-slow-motion is, there should be a little more punch to your plot. Have your hero wonder if his/her power should be used for good or evil, throw in a sense of longing (many heroes are loners or have watched loved ones perish) or what the heck, give your supervillain an alter ego!

Inspiration can come from superheroes other than those with their own film franchises. Here are a few high-flying books you might get a kick from (of course, the way Hollywood works, many of these probably *will* have film adaptations by the time this book is published):

- The Bone series, by Jeff Smith
- The Babymouse series, by Jennifer L. Holm and Matt Holm
- The Captain Underpants series, by Dav Pilkey
- The Extraordinary Adventures of Ordinary Boy series, by William Boniface
- The Maximum Boy series, by Dan Greenburg
- *The Great Cape Rescue*, by Phyllis Shalant

5 Silly Questions
with Gordon Korman

JS: You wrote your first book, *This Can't Be Happening at Macdonald Hall*, when you were only 12 years old! When I was 12 I spent my days having soda-pop-chugging contests and daring friends to eat worms. What motivated the preteen Gordon to become a published author?

GK: It was a school project. Our teacher, who was actually a track and field coach, gave us the rest of the year to write "a novel." It was February. I guess I took him more literally than my fellow students. At the time, I happened to be the class monitor for Scholastic Book Clubs, so I sent my manuscript to the address on the order forms. (You can also find this story in the dictionary, under "fluke.")

JS: Your Island series *(Shipwreck, Survival, Escape)* is about a group of children who are stranded on a deserted island. That's a popular theme in entertainment these days, with *Survivor, Lost* and *Cast Away*. In order to compete, did you ever consider including an immunity idol volleyball named Wilson with mysterious numbers carved on it in one of your books?

GK: There was some seriously lucky timing with Island. I started on the series in March, and *Survivor* debuted that summer. *Cast Away* came at Christmas. True, I never thought of the volleyball thing, but since my characters were shipwrecked as a group, they had no need of inanimate objects to hang out with. And I included something that *Cast Away* missed — using Ian's glasses to start a fire. Tom Hanks could have done that with Helen Hunt's locket thingy. It would have saved him a lot of hassle.

JS: One of your book titles is doing the questioning for me: *Why Did the Underwear Cross the Road?*

GK: To get to the other side, obviously. When it comes to motivation, undergarments are very similar to poultry. This is a known fact.

JS: You've won many prestigious awards already, but I'd like to bequeath one more upon you: Best Book Title Ever, for *Your Mummy Is a Nose Picker*.

GK: Thanks. The *Nose Picker* books never managed to garner the audience of some of my other titles (I wonder why), and I'm sure this award will go a long way to getting them the critical acclaim they deserve.

JS: I love the cover of one of your books in particular, which features a baby sporting a mohawk. Did you suggest a picture of a school principal with goth dreadlocks for the cover of *Schooled*?

GK: That was the first time a publisher ever used my idea for a book cover, so I'm particularly proud of it. I'm also responsible for the peace sign in the *Schooled* cover, but not the overall design. Some higher-ups in the publishing hierarchy nixed the dreadlocks, drat the luck. All the really cool ideas never see print.

Gordon Korman was born in Montreal, raised in Toronto and now lives on Long Island, New York. His novels (such as his contributions to the 39 Clues series) have reached bestseller lists and have also won many literary awards, including Joel A. Sutherland's Best Book Title Ever Award.

Don't Forget to Read (Duh!)

Non-Fiction Is Non-Boring

Libraries have them. So do bookstores.

I'm not talking about people who say "shush" too much. I'm talking about non-fiction sections.

Wait, wait, come back! Non-fiction is not something you need to avoid like the bubonic plague. (Interested in the bubonic plague? Read a non-fiction book about it!) There's more to the non-fiction section than reference books like math guides and dictionaries.

> My father gave me a dictionary for my birthday. I couldn't find the words to thank him.

Trust me, there are plenty of exciting non-fiction reads to be, um, read. Everyone has special interests and hobbies, and there has been a book published about virtually every special interest and hobby under the sun. (Interested in the sun? Read a non-fiction book about it!) Non-fiction books are an electrifying wealth of information, sure to spark the imagination of anyone with a pulse. (If you don't have a pulse, don't worry: there are non-fiction books for you, too. These days, it isn't hard to find "true" books about vampires and zombies.)

If your non-fiction interest has been piqued, but you don't know where to start, check online or ask your favourite librarian (if I'm busy with another customer, ask your *second* favourite librarian) for the list of winners from the Norma Fleck Award, the Silver Birch Award, the Hackmatack Award and the Red Cedar Award. All are packed with incredible non-fiction books and the books are, in turn, packed with incredible facts. Of course, there is a veritable sea of great

After a long night of water skiing, I love to relax with a good non-fiction book.

reading available at your library or bookstore and these award-winning books are only the tip of the iceberg. (Interested in icebergs? Read a non-fiction book about them!)

Looking to dive in to the non-fiction sea? Here are five of the coolest things I learned from reading five of my favourite non-fiction books:

1. A group of female Chinese runners did so well in the Summer Olympics of the 1990s that people began to wonder if they had used performance-enhancing drugs. Their coach claimed that no, they had not taken drugs, but instead had eaten soup and beverages made from turtle's blood and caterpillar fungus — yes, *caterpillar fungus* — to make them faster. Yum! (*Gold Medal for Weird*, by Kevin Sylvester)

2. Ancient Egyptian "dentists" would slice a mouse in half and place it on the patient's gum in an attempt to cure toothaches. Yum! (*Horrible Histories: Awful Egyptians*, by Terry Deary)

3. The first sets of dentures ever made were constructed with teeth taken from dead bodies. Not yum. Not yum at all. (*Boredom Blasters*, by Helaine Becker)

4. When a customer told a staff member that she believed the tales of ghosts occupying Deane House, a restaurant in Calgary, had been fabricated to attract more customers, her teacup levitated above the table. I'm betting she left the restaurant hungry. (*Haunted Canada: True Ghost Stories*, by Pat Hancock)

5. An American ice cream manufacturer once produced ketchup-flavoured ice cream, although the product was short-lived. What were they thinking? Perhaps the better question is why did the five cool facts I selected involve food, mouths and taste buds? I better go check out a non-fiction book on eating to try and find the answer! (*Transformed: How Everyday Things Are Made*, by Bill Slavin)

So the next time you're searching for a new book to read, take a look in the non-fiction section. You'll thank me. (Interested in me? Read a non-fiction book about it!)

The day they write a book about you is the day I quit the human race.

5 Silly Questions
with Hugh Brewster

JS: You wrote the Silver Birch Express Award-nominated book *Breakout Dinosaurs*. I've watched *Jurassic Park* countless times (at least twice), and when dinosaurs break out, people freak out. How would you remain calm during a dinosaur theme park malfunction?

HB: A little dinosaur knowledge might save me from becoming dinosaur lunch. The giant sauropods, like *Diplodocus*, for example, were plant eaters. So I'd know that I just had to keep out of their way. The worst they might do is stomp on me by accident. Same goes for *Triceratops* and all the duck-billed hadrosaurs like *Edmontosaurus*. I'd be a little worried about carnivorous predators like *Allosaurus* or *T. rex*. But we know they had a pretty acute sense of smell. So I might douse myself in really bad cologne and wear a polyester leisure suit. If that wouldn't scare all the predators it would probably keep the female ones at a distance.

JS: The subtitle of *Breakout Dinosaurs* is *Canada's Coolest, Scariest Ancient Creatures Return!* Do the coolest dinosaurs form exclusive cliques, drive expensive cars and shoot spitballs at the geekiest dinosaurs?

HB: Well, there sure were some geeky dinosaurs. *Stegosaurus*, for example, was big and slow and kinda stupid, with a brain the size of a walnut. The ankylosaurs — the armoured dinosaurs that looked like walking tanks — were also slow and a bit dull. They also had wicked farts that would not have made them popular prom dates. But the cool dinos like *T. rex* didn't shun the geeks. They ate them.

JS: Privilege, prestige, power, parties — these are only some of the highlights of being a princess, as discussed in *To Be a*

Princess. Tell me, as you lie awake at night dreaming of being a princess, which part of the royal lifestyle do you long for the most?

HB: Well the jewels are hard to beat. One Russian princess liked to keep bowls of rubies, diamonds and emeralds around the palace just so she could run her hands through them. And entering a giant ballroom covered in glittering jewels and having everyone bow to the floor as you pass by — that I could get used to. But if you're not careful the ordinary people start to hate you. And they might just chop off your head. So that's something princesses have to watch out for.

JS: How did you come up with a whopping 882½ questions in *882½ Amazing Answers to Your Questions About the Titanic?* I have a hard enough time coming up with five for these silly interviews!

HB: Easy. Just think of *Jeopardy.* Start with the answer and then make it a question. Let's take the dogs. We know there were dogs on the *Titanic.* So what happened to them? Did they all drown? Were they locked in their kennel? Did people take them in the lifeboats? Only 878½ more questions to go and you have a book!

JS: I've got to turn my silly switch off for a moment. You're perhaps best known for your books about Canada's involvement in World War I and II, *On Juno Beach, At Vimy Ridge* and *Dieppe: Canada's Darkest Day of World War II.* As the proud grandson of two late World War II veterans, I'd like to thank you for keeping these major events fresh in the minds of today's youth. What has been the most rewarding experience for you in writing these books?

HB: Meeting the soldiers who were there. They're all amazing men — and women. My mother (now 92) was an army nurse. I showed her the Dieppe book and she couldn't finish it. "I nursed those boys," she said, "it's too hard." Many of the World War II veterans didn't talk about the war until they were in their 80s. Now they want their stories told before they die. Sometimes they tell me things they haven't told anyone in over 60 years. Sometimes they cry, and I cry, too. I went to the 65th anniversary ceremonies at Dieppe with my young nephew. We stood on the pebbled beach below the chalk cliffs where almost a thousand Canadians died. When the band played "O Canada" and the old men saluted their lost comrades, the tears just flowed. It's the most moving experience I've ever had as a Canadian.

Hugh Brewster is living his dream, creating books about history. His ability to think of 882½ questions on a single topic — let alone his talent for keeping important historical events alive in our memories — is worthy of great admiration. And don't forget to check out 882½ Amazing Answers to Your Questions About the Titanic *to find out what happened to all the pooches!*

Nuts and Bolts

How Many Editors Does it Take to Change a Light Bulb?

Now that you've survived the storm in your brain and overcome writer's block to pen the first draft of your magnum opus (you go, you!), it's time to edit your work. I can't stress this enough: editing is one of the most important stages of writing. If it weren't for editing, I'd look like an incredibly huge moron.

To prove my point, I've asked Jennifer, my editor extraordinaire, to leave her editing marks in for the rest of this chapter. Starting now!

Some people balk at the idea of editing, preferring the act of writing. But editing is the bee's knees! [*Editor's Pen: How old are you? Nobody says "the bee's knees" anymore.*] I've got ~~eight~~ seven tips to make editing a snap, so from one to ~~six~~ seven, here they are:

1. **Concentrate.** Have you ever read an *I Spy* or *Where's Waldo* book? They require concentration, don't they? So does proper editing. Give a warm glass of milk to your cell phone and switch off that crying baby. [*EP: I'm 99.9% sure you mixed these two up.*]

2. ~~b~~ **Print.** If you've been using a computer to write, print out a copy of your story. It's easier to spot mistakes on paper than on screen. And if you read the story out loud to yourself, your ear might pick up a few more errors.

3. **Words.** Some are easy to mix up, such as then/than, accept/except, and there/their/they're. Words that sound alike ~~butt~~ but have different meanings are called homoni . . . homona . . . [*EP: homonyms*]

4. **Punctuation.** Don't get so caught up checking every single word in your story that you forget to check that you've used correct punctuation, such as commas, periods, question marks, exclamation marks and on and on or else your sentences will be way too long and

people will have a really hard time following your train of thought and it will be difficult to understand your meaning and that of course would be a bad thing. [*EP: Run-on sentence.*]

5. Backwards. Read your story from the final word to the first. It will sound like Chewbacca has written it, [*EP: You mean Yoda. If Chewie had written it, it would sound like "Raaarghhh growkk yawrrrk," not like someone talking backwards.*] but it will stop your brain from automatically correcting mistakes and filling in missing words.

6. Books. Two of them, the dictionary and the thesaurus, are great editing tools. Take some time to make sure you've spelled difficult words right, and that you've used them correctly, with the dictionary. If you're repeating the same words over and over, use the thesaurus to get some fresh ideas. The spell-check function on your computer, while not completely reliable, will also alert you to many of your mistakes. [*EP: Hey! Great section! I don't actually have anything to add, alter or delete. Perhaps that's because I suggested you add this section during the editing process, but congratulations all the same!*]

7. Someone, er, else. [*EP: You've painted yourself into a corner by beginning each tip with one word, haven't you?*] Have a friend or a family member edit your story for you. You'll be amazed by how many mistakes there still are, regardless of how many times you've gone over it yourself! [*EP: You can say that again.*]

A final note on criticism: it should always be positive. Whether you're editing your own words or someone else's, it's important to treat the writer with respect. Criticism can be extremely helpful and supportive, but it can also be destructive and hurtful. Make sure to point out ways to improve the writing instead of simply pointing out what is wrong, and always tell the writer, even if it's yourself (*especially* if it's yourself!), what he or she did right. [*EP: Ah, man . . . you're starting to make me feel bad. All right, I promise to only be positive from here on out and to not call you any more names.*]

Now you've seen what one chapter of this book looked like before my editor corrected it. I Hope, I didn't come off looking *too* moronik. [*EP: That's "moronic," you moron . . . I know, I know — I promised not to call you any more names, but you set yourself up too well, Sutherland!*] And that's the end of this chapter. Until the next chapter, goodbye!

[*EP: Forgetting something?*]

Um, I don't think so.

[*EP: Take another look at this chapter's title.*]

"How Many Editors Does it Take to Change a Light Bulb?" All right, what of it?

[*EP: Did you ever, oh, I don't know . . . answer that question?*]

Right! Thank you, Jennifer. How did I miss that?

[*EP: Hey, I'm impressed you even remembered to include this chapter at all! Remember how in your first draft you forgot to include Gordon Korman's completed interview?*]

Yeah! He would have been furious! Good thing you caught that and he'll never know how close he came to being left out. Anyway, how many editors does it take to change a light bulb? Only one, but first she has to rewire the entire building. Get it? Because editors are compelled to change everything, even if it's not necessary. Ha, ha, ha!

I like this editor!

[*EP: Good one.*]

5 Silly Questions
with Barbara Haworth-Attard

JS: On writing the historical fiction novel *A Trail of Broken Dreams* (part of the Dear Canada series), you've said, "it has always struck me how emotionally people are the same. No matter if it is the 1800s or the 2000s, love, jealousy, fear or hatred have no time or geographic boundaries." Let's go in the other direction and say it's the 2200s. Will people still have the same emotions, or will they be too distracted by piloting their jet packs safely (I'm sure having a seagull fly into one's face in mid-air wouldn't tickle) to be concerned with love, jealousy and all that other stuff?

BHA: Yes, I truly believe there will still be coveting, envy, passion, jealousy, hatred, no matter what the era or the distractions. They will perhaps, though, take different forms, such as bullying becoming an Internet problem, hatred being expressed in text messages. A jealous lover will fly his jet pack into his ex-girlfriend's jet pack out of revenge and always there is that underlying cause of so many wars — greed for what the other person has — be it land, money or person.

JS: I've read that you're a self-taught writer, and that you've read all 800 books on writing in the London Public Library. Aside from a slight shake in my knees at the thought of my own book on writing's chances of standing out from the crowd (800 in London alone!), I'm amazed you found the time to read so many books. Has your library card melted yet from overuse?

BHA: When I was young and considering my career options (which my mother decided for me by getting me a filing job in an insurance company when I was 17) being a writer was not even on the radar. I myself thought all those books in the library I loved had been written by dead or English people. To this day I find many people think I have a nice hobby, and

I have fielded comments like, "Someone has a lot of time on their hands." Or, "I always wanted to be a writer in my spare time, too." Okay, that sounds a little bitter, but it's true. Let me announce to the world that I have paid my dues! I worked for a law firm, raised my two sons, kept house and compulsively wrote in what little spare time I had. I never suggest anyone quit their job to become a writer. In fact, I couldn't write if I didn't have lots of other stuff tugging at my attention. I think it is wonderful that most universities now offer creative writing classes. Oh, I didn't read 800 books — I read the books in the 800 section (the writing section) of the library — more like maybe 120.

JS: *To Stand On My Own: The Polio Epidemic Diary of Noreen Robertson* is your second addition to the Dear Canada series. Diary books are so hot right now, thanks, in part, to Greg Heffley. But something tells me Noreen Robertson isn't a wimpy kid. Or someone who gets the Cheese Touch. Or a stick figure. Right?

BHA: Noreen is an ordinary kid — like every kid out there — who discovers that when the chips are down and when she needs it most, there is a lot of strength inside to rely on. She learns that it is okay to whine and cry and have a self-pity party for a while, but then she picks herself up and tackles her problems head-on.

JS: In *TruthSinger* and *WyndMagic*, Nathan hears songs that reveal the hidden truth about a person. What if he looked at me and heard — and I use this term loosely — the Greatest Hits of Britney Spears? What would that say about my psyche?

BHA: Hmmm . . . I don't know you well enough to comment on your psyche. I think what I was getting at with those books was that we all wear masks, different ones at different times, including myself. We might present ourselves one way, but we're really another way. And, scary thought that it is, there are people out there amongst us whose true selves are so hidden, such as serial killers, it is difficult to discern who they really are. Having said that, on the whole, though, I think with me, what you see is what you get.

JS: You have the uncanny ability to get into the heads of a wide array of characters from many time periods and all walks of life (a girl in post-World War II Canada, a boy living on the streets in contemporary Toronto). For *Haunted*, how did you get into the head of Dee, a girl with the ability to see spirits from the afterlife, as well as their deaths, without giving your family the willies?

BHA: I think I'm fairly empathetic. I cry easily at movies and books, can relate to them on a personal level and try to bring that to my own stories. Dee is just an ordinary teenage girl, with a little added something. I just try to look at the world from within their eyes. Okay, I'm weird. And I don't give my family the willies because I don't discuss what I'm writing with them. I'm mom, mother-in-law and wife to them, which is how it should be. Oh, yeah, I am extraordinarily nosy and curious about people. I love hearing their stories.

Barbara Haworth-Attard is a native of Elmira, Ontario, currently residing in London, Ontario with her family. June 1995 saw the publication of her first junior novel, Dark of the Moon. *Since then she has written 12 novels in the historical fiction, fantasy and contemporary genres for middle-grade and young adult readers. No doubt about it, she has paid her dues.*

61

Game On

Write to the Future

We're going back in time! Don't step on any bugs or you might warp the space-time continuum, alter history and cause everyone to be enslaved by giant lizards back in the present. Or something like that. I don't know, time travel is confusing. Just don't touch anything!

Creating a time capsule is fun the whole family can have together. Follow these steps for a safe, giant lizard-free project:

1. Find a capsule. Old cookie tins, glass jars and plastic containers will work well. Make sure it has a lid that seals tight, because although water is our friend, it is a time capsule's enemy. You don't want to open your time capsule after a few years and find it's filled with a soggy pile of mush that used to be your special mementos. Write your name and the date on the outside of the capsule. Also, give the time capsule a witty name, like "Time Capsule."

2. Write a letter to your future self. Where do you see yourself in one, five or ten years? What are your hopes, dreams and aspirations? What would you like to be when you're older?

3. If you have a pet, write a letter on its behalf (pets have a notoriously difficult time holding pens). List their likes and dislikes. List their favourite human, which is obviously you. Sign the letter by dipping their paw in non-toxic paint and pressing it to the paper. If your pet is a dog or a cat, that is. It would be tough to do the same for a goldfish. Oh, and make sure to clean your pet's paw afterwards. I can't stress enough how important that is.

4. Add a few items of special meaning. This could be anything: a hockey card, a story or poem you wrote, a

small toy, your lucky sock (washed, preferably). Write a list of the items and briefly describe why they are special to you.

5. Seal it up and bury it somewhere on your property or in a rustic area you're reasonably sure will not be developed anytime soon. There would be nothing worse than going to the forest where you buried your time capsule and finding a Walmart in its place. And then finding out they're fresh out of story ideas!

6. Wait however long you decided to wait, then go dig it up and have fun looking at all your old stuff. Look over both shoulders for giant lizards, then safely head back home.

I think you need to go on a diet. You're getting too heavy for your scales.

You're a regular stand-up chameleon.

If your memory is anything like mine (that is to say, like a goldfish's), you'd be wise to draw a map to the location of your buried time capsule. Take your map to the next level and give it a more authentic, antique look. Dip it in soya sauce to give it an old appearance, and ask an adult to burn a little bit of the edges. Pirates were always accidentally burning their stuff. Pirate mothers didn't teach their pirate babies to not play with matches.

The only kind o' treasure I hate be lost treasure!

5 Silly Questions
with Richard Scrimger

JS: In your book, *From Charlie's Point of View*, the main character's dad is accused of bank robbery. Was this secretly inspired by true life events?

RS: Absolutely. My Uncle Jim is currently doing 10 years less a day for bank robbery. (He got the day taken off because he bowed to the judge and called her "Miss." She was flattered.)

JS: If you had to have an alien live in your nose, like in *The Nose from Jupiter*, would you pick (pun intended) ET or Yoda?

RS: I'd definitely go with Yoda — a much better conversationalist. (Rhinitis, you have.) For me, though, the key question about an alien in my nose is: would Sigourney Weaver be there to help me deal with it?

JS: If you were an alien, whose nose would you want to live in? Why?

RS: It's getting scary out there. Everyone is getting smaller noses! Why don't celebrities build extensions? Big noses are cool, I tell you. I like a bit of room to stretch out in. What I'd LOVE is to move into Pinocchio's nose, and get him to tell me lies all day so I could fit in my sectional couch. It won't fit into my apartment now.

JS: In *Eugene's Story*, Eugene makes his sister shrink and vanish so that he can finish telling his story without being interrupted. Do you have any special methods of dealing with obstacles to your writing?

RS: My method for dealing with obstacles is to turn them into building blocks. If I break an egg, I make an omelet. If I break a dozen eggs, I make a big omelet and invite my friends.

JS: You also wrote the very funny book, *The Way to Schenectady*. Do you have any other hard-to-pronounce titles in the works?

RS: My next book is called *Me & Death*. I have NO idea how to pronounce "&." Maybe "hn" or "uhn." Maybe "pn" like in pneumonia.

Richard Scrimger lives in Cobourg, Ontario, where he is hard at work trying to figure out how to pronounce "&." He has also written a few other books of varying degrees of pronunciation difficulty. He has four teenaged children, a collection of speeding tickets and, usually, a puzzled expression.

Write Like an Alien

Space, the final frontier. But science fiction ("sci-fi" to people who are too lazy to say complete words) doesn't have to be about distant planets and alien races. It could also take place here on Earth and deal with time travel, cloning or robots run amok. Or bring the aliens to our planet and have them blow up some world famous landmarks, as aliens love to do.

Once you're done with all the big stuff, would you mind swinging past my school?

Here are a few points to consider to take your sci-fi (I'm lazy) story to infinity . . . and beyond!

1. **Start thinking about your topic.** Writing science fiction requires knowing a little bit about science fact (if you shorten that to "sci-fa," you are officially the laziest person on the planet . . . perhaps on any planet). Read some science books and magazines, scan newspaper headlines and talk to anyone you know who keeps up-to-date with the latest science news. You never know where you will find the perfect idea, so keep your eyes and ears open.

2. Once you've settled on a topic, stretch the idea further by asking yourself "what if?" Say you read an article about the discovery of water on Mars, but what if it wasn't really water — maybe it's a water-based, shape-shifting alien life form?

3. If your story will be set on a distant planet, think about what the planet is like. Is it covered in water, sand or tropical forest? If your story will have aliens in it, picture what they look like and what type of technology they have. Are they short, tall, skinny, fat? Do they have advanced ray guns and flying saucers or are they very primitive?

4. Speaking of aliens, they don't always need to be mean and violent. They don't even have to blow up world famous landmarks! They could be friendly like E.T., wise like Yoda or even take up residence in your nose like Norbert in *The Nose from Jupiter*.

5. Decide what the conflict of the story will be. It could be man versus man, man versus technology or man versus nature. In a nutshell, if man is fighting something, you've got a conflict, and then you've got a story.

Reading a sci-fi novel or two might help inspire you to write your own. Here are some great books to read to see where other authors have piloted their spaceships within the genre:

- *The Nose from Jupiter*, by Richard Scrimger
- *Animorphs*, by K.A. Applegate
- *Cloning Miranda*, by Carol Matas
- *The Mysterious Benedict Society*, by Trenton Lee Stewart
- *The City of Ember*, by Jeanne DuPrau
- *When You Reach Me*, by Rebecca Stead

5 Silly Questions
with Carol Matas

JS: The first volume of The Ghosthunters trilogy, written with Perry Nodelman, is *The Proof that Ghosts Exist*. The second and third volumes are *The Curse of the Evening Eye* and *The Hunt for the Haunted Elephant*. If an evening eye is cursed and an elephant is haunted, is that definite, 100% proof that ghosts exist? Or could the eye be a little sleepy in the evening and the elephant simply spooked by a mouse?

CM: This answer is from both Perry and me: as it happens, the eye is actually a large emerald and the elephant is actually a carving. So if the eye is sleepy or the elephant is worried about a mouse, then that does prove ghosts exist.

JS: On one of your blogs, you said you've "never sent off a manuscript without getting sick." What compels you to suffer such a stomach-spinning, porcelain throne-worshiping, green-faced hardship time after time?

CM: The answer to that question is easy: it's my heartfelt conviction that after all that work, all that research, all that thinking, after putting my heart and soul into the book, after all that the editor will turn around and say, "This book stinks!" And that's actually happened to me a couple times. The funny thing is, after it happened, I said, "No! It doesn't!" And went and found a different publisher who liked it as much as the first one hated it. More usual is the reaction that it's basically good but needs work. So I groan a little and then get back to work making it better. I am waiting anxiously as I write this for the reaction to my latest book! (AAAARG!)

JS: In one of your books, a girl wakes up with the ability to read minds. This reminds me of my own brush with the paranormal. One day a woman approached my desk and asked where the books about psychic abilities were. "I can read minds," she informed me. I don't know why, but the first thought that popped into my head was, "Oh, so can I." (FYI: I can't.) Her eyes widened, her jaw dropped and she said, "You too?" True story. So let's get to the question: if you didn't believe in telepathy before hearing my story, do you now? (And, I'm a little afraid to ask, but can *you* read minds?)

CM: OK. Why did she need to ask where the psychic books were if she was truly psychic? Hah! Here's the thing though. I actually do have some psychic ability. I was unaware of it myself until my daughter's first date. I predicted how long the relationship would last and how it would end and was right up to the exact day. This happened with each new boyfriend until she stopped letting me predict as I was always right. Were these self-fulfilling prophecies? I don't think so because even after I stopped telling her my predictions — I whispered them to my husband — they were always right. It ended with me predicting the man she would marry and when she would marry, and it all came to pass! And that actually is a true story.

JS: In response to the question of where you get your ideas, one of the sources you've listed is "talking to a friend." Do your friends receive a percentage of your books' royalties, and if not, what's your secret for retaining friendships?

CM: My friend Janeen is an artist and was doing a series on the witch burnings. One day on the phone she told me all about what happened to women back then and I knew immediately I had to write about it. One of the reasons being that feminism has become such a dirty word with young women and I wanted them to see that feminists were and are brave, and fight for all of us. And if you need any reminding just look at many places in the world right now, never mind centuries ago, where women have no rights at all. Regarding retaining friendships: people ask me why I write so many books. Isn't it obvious? So I can dedicate them to various friends and thus keep them indebted to me forever! Yes, a dark and sneaky plan!

JS: You wrote a trilogy about a girl who is cloned: *Cloning Miranda, The Second Clone* and *The Dark Clone*. If you had a clone, would you use it for good (to write twice as many books), or for evil (to watch twice as many reality shows)?

CM: Oh, that's so easy! Evil! Reality shows! I am addicted to *So You Think You Can Dance,* have watched all seasons of *Idol* and have seen just about every house-buying, house-fixing show that exists. And then there's *The Bachelorette* but let's not even go there.

Carol Matas has written 40 books for children, teens and young adults, in a wide array of genres. All the more impressive considering her reality TV show addiction!

Don't Forget to Read (Duh!)

Libraries: They're Not Just for "Ssshhhers" Anymore

Public library: those two words can evoke feelings of dread and revulsion as strong as the word "dentist" for some. The fear of returning a book late, of being chased down by the library policeman or of being *ssshhhed* out of the building still affects many.

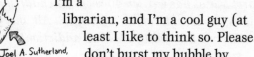

But that's the public library of yesterday. The public library of today is a cool place to hang out. I'm a

Joel A. Sutherland, Cool Librarian

librarian, and I'm a cool guy (at least I like to think so. Please don't burst my bubble by telling me otherwise).

Many libraries today have modern collections, such as DVDs, CDs, video games and graphic novels (at the risk of being ostracized for revealing top secret librarian information, calling comic books "graphic novels" makes librarians more comfortable about stocking them), and they host exciting events such as pizza parties and video game tournaments. And yes, we still have good ol' fashioned books.

Remember how we talked about dealing with distractions earlier in the book? Let's say you've done everything humanly possible to block out the wails of that crying baby at home, but it's still far too loud to get any work done there. Libraries have plenty of quiet areas that are perfect for writing and reading. Just don't sit too close to the storytime room — it can get pretty rowdy. As an added bonus, you'll then be smack dab in the middle of the best place to complete any research needed for your book!

Here's another problem many writers face while trying to work at home: everybody wants to hop on the computer at the same time that you've been struck by an inspirational lightning bolt and need to write. Your younger brother wants to play games, your older sister wants to update her Facebook status, your mom wants to watch viral Youtube videos and your dad wants to craft the perfect 140-character tweet about his model train set. Sound familiar? Then it's time to use the computers at the library!

One final note: while you're there, take a look for advertisements and flyers for writing groups and workshops. Many are held in libraries, and that could be a great way to meet other people with similar interests that can help you with your latest magnum opus. Or at least they might be able to explain exactly what a "magnum opus" is (and if you find out, please let me know — I have no idea what it means, but I feel it makes me sound smart to drop it into casual conversations).

So don't forget to check out your local library!

5 Silly Questions
with Ted Staunton

JS: Your first book, *Puddleman*, is about a kid who jumps in a sandbox, turns into a mud monster and then craves sandwiches. Any plans for a sequel, say, about a kid who jumps into a mudbox, turns into a sand monster and then craves mudwiches?

TS: Aw, mannnn . . . where are those suggestions when I need them? Except for eggplant, liver and asparagus (did I spell that right? I hate it so much I never even read it), I am a big food fan. Instead of mud pies my next picture book is about how a little brother figures out a way to keep his snacks when his big sister starts hogging them. Pass the gravy.

JS: In your popular Morgan series, such as *Morgan Makes Magic*, there is a character known as the Godzilla of Grade Three who inspires fear in all her classmates. Were you terrorized as a child by bullies, perhaps nicknamed the King Kong of Grade Two or the Stay Puft Marshmallow Man of JK?

TS: Hey, back when I was in school there were tough guys who'd stayed in grade eight so long they were old enough to drive. I was never bullied, though. I was 9 feet tall and weighed 400 pounds, making me the biggest liar you ever saw.

JS: I love the Monkey Mountain series (*Two False Moves* to *Trouble with Girls*), and I'd love to live on a mountain named after an exotic animal. Is it a real place? Do you know of any other alliterative alps I could visit? Maybe Parrot Pinnacle or Scorpion Summit?

TS: Monkey Mountain is a real place in my town. It's a ravine that's used as a short cut on the way to high school. Why is a hole in the ground called a mountain? That's Port Hope for you. The cool part is no one knows how it got the name "Monkey" either. One legend has it that in the 1800s monkeys escaped from a travelling circus and hung out there in the woods. These days the only monkey business is whatever high schoolers get up to. (Don't ask.) For your vacation I'd suggest Godzilla Gorge, instead, for a monstrously good time.

JS: *Hope Springs a Leak* follows the adventures of Sam Foster in his small Canadian town, the fictional Hope Springs, which is filled with colourful inhabitants. Wait a minute . . . you live in a small Canadian town, the factual Port Hope, which is filled with colourful inhabitants. Is this just a crazy coincidence?

TS: You promised not to tell. Except for the fact that they are exactly the same, Port Hope and Hope Springs have nothing in common. Nothing. Nada. Zilch. Are you trying to get me in trouble with my neighbours or what? Say, I wonder what they're up to . . .

JS: You also write for a children's non-fiction series, The Dreadful Truth, which examines Canadian history. The first two books, *Confederation* and *Building a Railway,* are quite fascinating and funny (with great illustrations to boot) . . . hardly dreadful at all! Do you have any plans to write another book in this series, and if so, can you promise that the subject matter will raise the dread quotient?

TS: You want dread? You've got it. The next book in the series (*Canadian Crime*) is a history of crime in Canada, *bwah-ha-ha.* It's stuffed with murderers, swindlers, robbers, rebels, people who stole door knockers and a couple of pirates. Read it if you dare.

Ted Staunton has written more than 25 books for children and young adults, and has won numerous awards. He followed Canadian Crime *with* The Northwest Passage *and* Gold Rush, *and I'm happy to report all contain an appropriate amount of dread. He lives in Port Hope, Ontario. (Or is that Hope Springs?)*

Nuts and Bolts

In a Bind? Bind Your Own Books!

You've written an incredibly moving, thrilling, hilarious tale. You've edited it to the point of perfection. Now it's time to show off your writing to the world by creating a beautifully crafted book!

First, you're going to need a cover. Have you heard the expression, "Never judge a book by its cover?" It's a wonderful sentiment, and it definitely applies to things like, say, people (just because a person looks a certain way, doesn't mean they necessarily *are* that way). But when it comes to actual books and actual covers, it's human nature to judge one by the other.

So you want to make sure your cover is visually striking and reflects the nature and topic of your book. Here are a few suggestions:

1. If you're a budding artist, this is a great way to share your talent with the world.

2. If you're a computer whiz, put your graphic art knowledge to good use.

3. But hey, if you're like me and are — how shall I put this nicely? — an atrocious artist, have no fear! Keep your cover simple: the title and your name will suffice, either handwritten or typed on a computer.

4. Feel free to incorporate a photograph or two for a little pizzazz.

5. And finally, if you can think of a tagline (a short and snappy sentence that ties into the book's subject matter), feel free to add it somewhere on the cover, too.

Next, it's time to bind the book:

1. Make sure your pages are all in order and stack them together.

2. For the front and back covers, it's best to use construction paper or another type of thick paper. If you want it to be especially durable, try cardboard.

3. If you use cardboard, you can cover it in coloured paper, wallpaper, fabric, felt or anything else you have at hand, and then glue your cover (or draw it straight on) to the covered cardboard.

4. Place the pages in between the covers and use a hole punch to punch holes (what a cleverly named tool) along the left-hand side of the book.

5. Weave a short length of string or ribbon through the holes and tie the ends together at the top of the book, cutting the extra bits off. Don't make it too tight or too loose — like Goldilocks' preference of porridge, chair and bed, it should be "just right." You want to make sure your readers can turn the pages without ripping them.

If my bed isn't just right, I suffer from nightbears.

Finally, don't forget to add all the little things that you typically see in your favourite books. Before your story you could write an acknowledgements page, a dedication and a copyright page (a simple "Copyright © [fill in the year] by [fill in your name]" will suffice), and you can end the book with an author's bio.

So as to not repeat myself — I'd hate to repeat myself — I won't bother explaining what to include in all of these sections. I simply won't explain what to include in all of these sections, since you can flip to the ones in this very book to see some valuable examples — yes, flip to the ones in this very book to see some valuable examples! (Did I repeat myself? I didn't repeat myself, did I? Did I?)

Once again calling them valuable, eh? Mister, you've got an odd sense of value.

By the way, you automatically own the copyright of your work as soon as you've written it. How cool is that?

So what is copyright? It's a form of protection that gives you the sole right to do (or to allow others to do) a number of things with your creation, such as making and distributing copies, displaying or performing your work and adapting the work for other media. The power! THE POWER!

5 Silly Questions
with Eric Wilson

JS: You're famous for the Tom and Liz Austen series of mystery books set in popular Canadian locations, such as *The Kootenay Kidnapper* and *Escape from Big Muddy*. But one of the books is set in an American location, *Disneyland Hostage*. Never heard of it. Why forgo mega-famous Canadian settings for an obscure American one?

EW: A lot of readers have suggested I might have used Canada's Wonderland instead of Disneyland. Next time I'll know better!

JS: My family lives in Ottawa. One of your books is titled *Vampires of Ottawa*. Should I pack some garlic and wooden stakes next time I visit Ma and Pa?

EW: Some long johns for winter weather might be more appropriate. I was born in Ottawa myself but eventually escaped to Victoria, where I met my dear wife Flo.

JS: *Code Red at the Supermall* takes place in the West Edmonton Mall, a real place that has sharks, rollercoasters, waterslides, a submarine and close to 1000 stores. Did you spend much time there researching the novel, and if so, was that the greatest job ever or was that the greatest job ever?

EW: Researching the mall was indeed a lot of fun, but walking those endless marble corridors did give me very tender tootsies.

JS: I recently learned that Winnipeg has been declared the "Slurpee Capital of the World." (Aside: my respect for the city immediately skyrocketed. End of aside.) Don't worry, I'm not going to ask you why it's the capital of Slurpees, but rather if *Terror in Winnipeg* is about the world's worst case of brain-freeze?

EW: On a serious note, I was disappointed when sales of this title climbed much higher following the 9/11 disaster.

JS: I've got my metal detector, flashlights and blueprints ready to go, but before I head into Toronto I need to ask — is *The Lost Treasure of Casa Loma* still lost? (I hate found treasure, unless it's found by yours truly — I'm very piratical in that regard.)

EW: Casa Loma is truly a Canadian treasure so it will always be waiting for tourists to discover.

Eric Wilson is a successful writer of mystery stories for children, having sold more than 1.5 million books in Canada alone and another 1 million books in 10 languages around the globe. He currently lives in British Columbia, where "long johns" aren't a necessity on a day-to-day basis.

Game On

Silly Shout-Out Storytelling

For this game, the sillier you're feeling the better. Having spent this much time in my company, I doubt this is going to be a problem.

1. Sit in a circle and begin telling your friends a simple story: "I woke up on a completely normal day in my completely normal bed. The sun was shining and the birds were chirping. I stretched, yawned and walked downstairs."

2. Then, build up to a twist: "The smell of bacon and eggs was wafting from the kitchen. My mother was standing before the stove, her back to me. But as she turned around, I discovered that it wasn't my mother standing there, but . . . a . . . _____ . . . WEARING MY MOTHER'S HOUSECOAT!"

3. When you come to the blank, pause and have one of your friends shout out the first silly thing that pops into their head: "A KANGAROO!"

4. Then it's up to the person on your left to continue the story until they get to another silly shout-out moment. Then the storyteller role passes to the person on their left, and on and on until you reach a satisfyingly silly conclusion.

Why is a kangaroo wearing your mother's housecoat and cooking bacon and eggs in your kitchen? You'll have to shout-out sillies to find out.

I was hiding from my kid. Because it was raining, he was playing inside.

Before you know it, you and your friends will have created a funny new story! This is also a great way to pass the time on long car rides! Come to think of it, it could also work on short airplane flights or medium-length boat trips. Sorry, I have no idea how to pass the time on the following:

- brief bicycle tours
- prolonged hang-gliding soars
- average-length piggyback rides

5 Silly Questions
with Robert Paul Weston

JS: Your blog asks the questions, "Zorgama-*what?!* Zorgama-*who?!*" I briefly considered stealing those questions to begin this interview but then I came to my moralistic senses. Stealing is wrong! So I did some serious research, learned everything I could about you and your writing career and, after much brainstorming, I've come up with the most perfectly original question of all time to ask you: Zorgama-*why?!*

RPW: When I was a kid, there were times you could open a regular newspaper and read headlines like "Strange lights spotted in the skies over Helsinki!" It seems like that sort of reporting (at least outside the pages of absurd tabloids) has all but vanished. Now, this isn't to say I believe in the Loch Ness Monster or anything, but observing the trend, I began to wonder if something had happened to all the sasquatches and sea monsters, to all the many creatures of myth. Perhaps, I thought, they were kidnapped! But by who? And *why?* You could say *Zorgamazoo* is one possible answer.

JS: Roses are red, violets are blue. Why write in rhyme, *Zorgamazoo?*

RPW: I wrote Zorgamazoo in rhyme because I had no idea what I was doing. Basically, the novel started out as an idea for an extended picture book (and, incidentally, there's no such thing; picture books have a standard length and publishers don't like to fool with it). By the time I figured out Zorgamazoo was much larger than I first had planned, I was well past the point of no return. Of course, I'm certainly glad I persevered!

JS: You've called *Zorgamazoo* a "read-aloud novel." As a librarian, I'm wondering if you've ever considered the effect your book has had on the quiet sanctity of our public libraries?

RPW: I think libraries ought to come equipped with special "Read-Aloud Rooms." Glassed-in, soundproof booths full of cushy chairs and a raised platform. Readers (and their adoring audiences) can sequester themselves in there and ham it up with a well-thumbed copy of *Zorgamazoo* . . . or, for that matter, any old book they like!

JS: *Dust City* revisits Little Red Riding Hood as the wolf's son begins to suspect his father was framed. When writing fractured fairy tales, is the pen still mightier than the sword? I'm thinking a two-handed broadsword would be more appropriate than an itsy-bitsy pen when some serious fracturing is in order.

RPW: With that book, I did some very serious fracturing, indeed, so the novel veers quite dramatically away from the medieval folktales that inspired it. As for the power of the pen, let's just say it's a lot mightier than it looks! Then again, maybe it's not for me to say. I write all my books with a mechanical pencil.

JS: You must be full of great writing advice, such as to be careful using computer spell-checkers . . . especially cents sum buoys and girls rely on it too fixe miss steaks ewe kin knot sea. Any other advice?

RPW: My best advice is this: when you're not writing, spend more time reading novels than doing anything else. Writing schools can teach you the myriad of discrete techniques used by writers, but they do little to help you internalize them. The best way to do that is with lots of reading. Internalizing technique is important because it means you won't have to think about it quite so much when you begin writing yourself.

Robert Paul Weston is the author of two books for young readers. He lives in Toronto, where he is working on book number three. During breaks from writing, he draws blueprints for the first public library Read-Aloud Room. He uses a mechanical pencil.

Write Like a Monster

"Boo!"

"I vant to suck your blood."

"Braaaiiinnnsss . . ."

"Grrraulphipouf!"

These are the famous (and in one case, completely made-up) catchphrases of popular monsters.

Lighthearted horror stories are a lot of fun and perfect to share while seated around a campfire on camping trips or at a Halloween party while munching on mounds of itty-bitty chocolate bars.

No candy for me — it goes straight to my hips. I prefer healthy snacks — like human beans.

I'll stick to junk food. An order of fish and ships, please!

Here are some pointers for breathing new *life* into the *undead* genre:

1. Make a list of everything that scares you. Include both fictional scares (vampires, mummies, werewolves) and real-life concerns (global warming, spiders, your French teacher). If you tap into something that truly terrifies you, chances are it will truly terrify others. However, if you have some irrational fears, it's probably best to leave them out — you want something the general population would be afraid of. Adding "dark alleys" to the list: good. Adding "lollipops" to the list: not so much.

If you're as easily spooked as I am, don't read this section!

2. Still stuck for ideas? Keep a notebook by your bed at night. Everyone has nightmares from time to time, which is never any fun. They can come in handy, however, if you jot them down when you wake up and turn them into scary stories.

3. Once you've settled on which fear you're going to write about, plot out the rest of the story. Your vampires, zombies and werewolves need someone to attack. How will the characters fight back? Will they prevail in the end? Although most readers generally prefer happy endings, horror is one of the few genres in which it's okay if the bad guys sometimes win.

4. Speaking of the characters, make them believable. And make the setting and the action real. Although you might be writing about completely make-believe monsters, the story needs to be grounded in reality in order for people to be scared by it.

5. There are plenty of moods and tones that can work effectively in horror, so make sure to settle on one and stick with it. A slow-building creepy ghost story, or a breathless action-driven zombie apocalypse adventure? A dark and disturbing psychological mystery, or a lighthearted tongue-in-cheek look at monsters' daily lives? The choice is yours, but it's difficult to mix moods and tones without leaving readers feeling unsettled. You don't want your story to have more split personalities than Dr. Jekyll. (Technically, he only had one — Mr. Hyde — but you get the idea.)

6. Be wary of violence. Yes, yes, I know, this is a horror story we're talking about, and a little violence and gore can be used effectively. But if your story has too much it will quickly become repetitive, gratuitous and boring. A lot blood is often a sign that the writer is covering up his or her lack of ideas. Use it sparingly, and the reader will constantly be alert and nervous, just waiting for the next attack to happen.

7. Avoid plots involving water-skiing, *Canadian Idol*-watching, giraffe-loving vampires. Since brainstorming the idea back in the early chapters of this book, I've written the first 20 pages of a novel about such a villain, and let's just say I'll be leaving this vampire out in the sun. Without sunscreen.

Guess you have more guts than I do.

Here are some popular horror books to give you something to howl about:

- *Bunnicula*, by Deborah and James Howe
- The Goosebumps series, by R.L. Stine
- *Wolf Pack*, by Edo van Belkom
- *Monsterology*, by Arthur Slade
- The Haunting of Derek Stone series, by Tony Abbott
- *The Wolves in the Walls*, by Neil Gaiman
- *Coraline*, by Neil Gaiman
- *The Graveyard Book*, by Neil Gaiman (he's a creepy guy)

5 Silly Questions
with Arthur Slade

JS: You penned both *Monsterology* and *Villainology,* but what about giving the good guys their due? Is it because *Heroology* looks weird and is difficult to pronounce?

AS: Yes, I approached my publishers about a *Heroology* book and they said they couldn't publish anything with a "roo" in it. In fact, they said they would rue the day they used a "roo" in the title. Then they went on a big tirade about "oology" and how silly it sounded. It was all a very odd and uncomfortable conversation. Thus, I didn't even get to pitch my next idea for a *Poo-ology* book, at all.

JS: Newton, a boy who is terrified of death by lightning (I can't blame him — what an unsavoury way to go), has six rules for survival in *Jolted: Newton Starker's Rules for Survival.* I'd like to recommend a seventh: if golfing when a lightning storm begins, hold up your 1-iron. Because even God can't hit a 1-iron. Is Newton the type to appreciate a little golf humour?

AS: Newton finds golf humour really funny. Actually he finds golf hilarious. He often watches golf on TV to see if the golfers get hit by lightning. So far he hasn't had any luck seeing an actual strike, though he does often yell at them, "when thunder roars, run indoors!" Newton actually owns a 1-iron but he uses it as a paperweight.

JS: *Invasion of the I.Q. Snatchers:* some would say that, instead of the third book in your Canadian Chills series, this is actually another name for these silly interviews. Agree or disagree?

AS: What was that? I don't know how to answer this question. The deeper I get into this interview the harder it is to think. IQ? Invasion? Where? What's happening? Can I have a Nanaimo bar?

JS: *Megiddo's Shadow,* your award-winning novel about a Canadian boy fighting the Turks in Palestine during World War I, must have required a boatload of research. Are you a traditionalist when it comes to research, visiting libraries and digging around dusty archives, or do you thank your lucky literary stars for the invention of Google?

AS: In order to do research for that book, I got on my horse and rode and rode and rode and still didn't get to the Middle East. I didn't even get to eastern Saskatchewan. So, instead I saddled up Google, dug in the spurs and went everywhere! Now that's a horse! I did go to a few libraries and the British Imperial War Museum, but a lot of my research was found by galloping Google. Hmmm, should I write a book called *Googleology?*

JS: Your hero from *The Hunchback Assignments* is named Modo, inspired by *The Hunchback of Notre-Dame's* Quasimodo. I flipped through my dictionary and learned that "quasi" means "Having a likeness to something; resembling." I then looked up the word "modo," but discovered it's not a word at all, at least not one recognized by Mr. Merriam-Webster. So I'm left wondering three things: what does "modo" mean to you, why is your hero no longer resembling it and did this question make any sense at all?

AS: Well, Quasimodo means "half-formed" and so the modo part of the name means "formed" so the real question is who formed Modo? Where does he come from? And who is shaping him now? Is it Mr. Socrates, the British lord who found him and is raising him as a spy? Or is it his genetic makeup? And what is his makeup? Does he wear makeup? Did this answer make any sense at all?

Arthur Slade became a full-time writer after the publication of his first novel, Draugr, *and he received the Governor General's Award for Children's Literature in 2001. His fans are eagerly awaiting the publication of* Poo-ology. *Well, my 7-year-old nephew and I are, anyway.*

Don't Forget to Read (Duh!)

Everybody Likes a Quitter

Thanks, Ernest.

Quit. A powerful word meaning to stop, cease or discontinue. To give up or resign. To let go. To relinquish.

An act which is frowned upon and despised so much that a well-known expression, "Nobody likes a quitter," has become as fashionable to say as "He was as mad as a mule munchin' on bumblebees," and "Don't whiz on the electric fence."

When it comes to reading and writing, however, this shouldn't be the case. Quitting shouldn't always be a bad thing.

Let's face it: not all books are created equal. Some just aren't as good as others. Nothing is quite as tiresome as slogging your way through a book you're not enjoying. So what's stopping you from stopping? If you've given it a good shot, it's okay to set aside a book that hasn't turned out to be your thing in favour of another one. Because really, there are so many books and so little time.

And if you've started writing a story that you initially loved, only to discover halfway through you're just not that into it anymore, put it aside and begin a new story. If you're not enjoying writing your story, chances are people won't enjoy reading it, either.

I'd like to propose that we, as a general collective, alter the previously mentioned expression. No, not "Don't whiz on the electric fence" — I think that one's pretty good as it is — but "Nobody likes a quitter." When it comes to reading (a book you're not enjoying) and writing (a story that has lost its magic), *everybody* likes a quitter.

Except for teachers — if you're reading a book you're not enjoying for a school report, it's probably best you finish it anyway.

Back to you, Ernest.

5 Silly Questions
with Helaine Becker

JS: Being both a boy and a bookaholic, I completed the "Which Kid's Book Character Are You?" quiz in *The Quiz Book for Boys*. Due to my preferences (vegetables, helping people, triple-fudge cake, working hard to get my look right and boxers), I discovered I'm Captain Underpants. I've fully embraced this role, but I'm afraid my new attire (cape, tighty-whiteys, nothing else) might not be appropriate for the Canadian winter. Would it be wrong to retake the quiz and lie about my answers to avoid hypothermia?

HB: Cheating is wrong, and you know that, Joel. Deal with it.

JS: That's too bad, I was hoping that with some new answers, I'd get Reese McSkittles, the sports-loving main character in your bestselling Looney Bay All-Stars series. By dubbing him Reese McSkittles, were you consciously, unconsciously or semi-consciously appealing to all the candy-craving children of the world who are fans of Reese's Pieces and Skittles?

HB: Totally, unashamedly intentional. What better way to signal my character is "sweet" and likeable? My son was completely aghast. He said, "Mom, how can you!? You're promoting unhealthy eating habits to children!" I replied, "Heck, they're not my kids."

JS: Did you ever discover what the big idea is when you wrote *What's the Big Idea?* I've been wondering the same thing pretty well all my life.

HB: You mean there IS a big idea? I thought it was just a clever title. Just kidding.

I don't actually think there is single big idea. There are only lots and lots of little tiny ideas that add up to some pretty boffo inventions and innovations — that's what you'd find out if you actually READ the book, Joel.

JS: As the author of *Are You Psychic?*, I'm assuming you're an expert in the paranormal world and extra-sensory perception. To prove it, can you tell me what my fifth and final question is going to be?

HB: When I started writing *Are You Psychic?* I had to do lots of research to find out what was going on out there in the world of ESP research. I was excited, because I wanted to find out that there were some really cool and unexplainable things happening in the universe. And I wanted to find out if I had any special powers that I hadn't noticed before, other than the uncanny ability to make my hair curl in freakish ways.

Alas, I discovered I have zero-zero-ZERO psychic abilities. I wouldn't know who was coming to the door, even if you announced yourself by phone, email and five-alarm sirens first. I have NO IDEA what anyone else is thinking at any given moment. I can make stuff move with my mind, but that's usually because I've knocked it over with my elbow first and it is going to land on my toe.

JS: Psych! I'm not going to end with a fifth and final question after all! I *will* end by saying I wish there was room for more than 5 silly questions, since I didn't even get to mention your other great fiction and non-fiction books, such as *Like a Pro, Funny Business, Mother Goose Unplucked, Mama Likes to Mambo, Boredom Blasters, Secret Agent Y.O.U., Science on the Loose, The Insecto-Files,* and *Magic Up Your Sleeve.* If I were a smarter man, I'd be able to think of some way to work those titles into this interview, but regrettably, I'm not . . . Can you think of a way to work them in? (Oh, no! I ended up ending with a fifth and final question! Why aren't I a smarter man? (Oh, no! ANOTHER question!))

HB: Oh, dahling Helaine, the *Mama* Who *Likes to Mambo*, the one with *Magic Up Your Sleeve*, maybe you can explain something about this *Funny Business* at which you are so, *Like, a Pro*. I've checked my *Insecto-Files*, and I've consulted with *Mother Goose Unplucked* and her *Secret Agent Y.O.U.*, but I still haven't been able to track down the mystery of your *Science* — it's clearly *On the Loose*. What makes you such a *Boredom Blaster*?

My answer: Being open to life, to adventure, to new experiences, new people, and enchiladas.

A woman of many talents, bestselling and award-winning author Helaine Becker lives in Toronto, Ontario. She is not only crazy for enchiladas, but ice cream, as well.

What? People didn't quit the book after you told them it was okay to do so? You're lucky Helaine Becker is so funny, witty and well spoken, Sutherland. You're lucky.

Nuts and Bolts

Party Time! Host Your Own Book Launch!

Why should adults have all the fun? You too can host a party to launch your freshly bound book.

A book launch is a great way to kick back, celebrate your literary achievement and scarf down some cookies. It's also an opportunity to let the world (or at least a few close acquaintances) know about your book's completion. Who knows? One or two people might even ask to buy a signed copy!

But you want to make sure your guests have a good time, so to ensure that fun is had by all, a little pre-party planning is in order. Here are some things to consider:

1. Create and send out homemade invitations. Write a short description of the book to let people know what the cause for celebration is and to entice them to come and find out more. Once you've got them hooked, make sure to tell them where to go and when, or else you might be partying by yourself. You might also want to set an RSVP date, so you can plan on how many cookies you'll need.

2. Make posters and banners to decorate your party room. Larger versions of your book's cover work nicely, or you can make some original artwork tied into the book to display on the walls. A poster alerting your guests to the

location of the cookies is probably a good idea as well. You want to create a party atmosphere, and it's hard to do that when your dad's picture of dogs playing poker is the only artwork on the wall.

3. Buy cookies. Or better yet, bake some cookies yourself. Seriously, I can't stress enough how important the cookies are.

4. Practise your signature. You're going to be asked for a lot of autographs — you're a star!

Now that it's time to party, here are some things you can do to entertain your guests:

1. Read a section of your book. But don't read the entire thing, and don't read the ending! You want to make sure that everyone will want to read the book on their own after the party.

2. Talk a little bit about why you wrote the book. What was your inspiration, did you do any research, is it based on a true story?

3. Play a game that's somehow tied into your book. If your book is about school, play a game of tag. If it's about canines, play a game of pin the tail on the dog. If it's about cookies, have a blindfolded cookie taste test. (Note: blindfold the guests, not the cookies.)

4. Take lots of pictures.

5. If you are selling copies of your book, ask someone to be in charge of sales. That way, you can focus on mingling with your guests instead of worrying about the cash. Just make sure you pick someone who's responsible enough for this task. Mothers, fathers and grandparents are ideal. Little brothers, not so much.

Above all else, have fun, and this will be a party that everyone will remember for a long time.

One additional note: adult authors often provide wine and cheese at these types of parties, but you can serve *grape juice* and cheese instead (and don't forget the cookies!). At the time of the printing of this book there was no minimum cheese-eating age, but you'd better double check just to make sure that hasn't changed.

5 Silly Questions
with Jeremy Tankard

JS: Typically I interview authors with many published books, but your first one has just been released. This is going to be a challenge for my brain, my mind and my head. Before you skip ahead (that would be cheating), how do you think I'll fare?

JT: Surely your brain and your mind are the same thing. I think you'll fare just fine — you'll have to do a lot less research than if I'd written 20 books. Think how few people will want to interview me then, "Well, I could interview Jeremy, but then I'd have to read, like, a million of his dumb books." This is easy, you only have to read one.

JS: The book in question, *Grumpy Bird*, has been garnering such great advance praise that I felt it necessary to snag you before you became a famous gajillionaire. What do you plan on doing with your first gajillion?

JT: At the moment I'm having a hard time imagining just how big a gajillion even is. It sounds like a lot more than 20. Possibly even more than 30. I promise I won't spend it all in the same place.

When Bird woke up, he was grumpy.

JS: Bird wakes up grumpy: too grumpy to eat, play or even fly. In one of the first illustrations (right), the branch under his nest is roasting a marshmallow over the sun. Is he grumpy because he ran out of chocolate and graham crackers?

JT: Have you ever tried roasting a marshmallow over the sun? It ain't easy! You'd be grumpy, too.

JS: In answer to a question on your website, you say that you don't own a TV. I'm confused. What do you point your furniture at?

JT: You can point furniture at pretty much anything. You'd be surprised. Why, just the other day I pointed a sofa at someone just to help me make a point. And when a friend asked me where the bathroom was I used a coffee table to point the direction. It's much more effective than pointing with, say, your finger. I think you should try it sometime.

JS: Back to books. You were the illustrator for a children's non-fiction book, *Procrastination: Deal with it All in Good Time*. For the many fans of Bird and his mood swings, can you reassure us that you're not a procrastinator and that a sequel is in the works?

JT: Hey, I'm procrastinating right now as I type this! Bird is proving to be more popular than I would have dreamed. A sequel is indeed in the works, but I can't say too much about it at the moment, as there isn't anything official to say. I can tell you about my second book though. It's called *Me Hungry*, from Candlewick Press. In fact I'm pointing a lamp at it right now just to emphasize how I feel about it.

Jeremy Tankard is a Toronto-based, award-winning artist. His illustrations have appeared in publications such as The New York Times *and* Time *magazine.* Grumpy Bird *is his first book,* Me Hungry, *his second. And, seeing as it's since been published, I feel it's safe to mention — er, I mean, point a lamp at — his third book:* Boo Hoo Bird.

Game On

Ready, Set, Draw!

It's said that a picture is worth a thousand words (but if your teacher asks for a thousand-word report, I wouldn't recommend handing in a single picture). Illustrations can add a new dimension to your stories. In fact, they can even become the driving force of your stories when you're creating manga or comic books.

But wait. Say you're like me. Did you see the vampire I drew for the brainstorming activity earlier in the book?

> I kinda liked that drawing. Had a certain *je ne sais quoi.*

If you're not good at drawing, here are some other methods you can play with to bring your words to life!

1. **Use modelling clay.** Using a piece of cardboard, spread a thin layer of modelling clay to serve as your background. Next, create people, animals, buildings and objects to layer on top of the background. Finally, use small tools — such as pencils, combs and forks — to "draw" details into the clay. If you do use a fork, make sure to clean it thoroughly afterwards. Plasticine doesn't taste all that great. Photograph your modelling clay illustrations and add the pictures to your book.

2. **Make a collage.** You can use magazines, newspapers, postcards, photographs, wallpaper, fabric, string, beads, seeds, feathers or anything else you can find that is relatively flat. Arrange them all on a piece of cardboard, and once everything looks just right, begin to glue the pieces down. It might get messy, but messy = fun.

3. **Make a sand drawing.** If you haven't run out of glue or

cardboard yet, try making an illustration with glue, then sprinkling sand over it. The sand will stick to the glue lines and suddenly you'll have an interesting piece of art. Add some more glue and then different colours of sand (which can be purchased in art supply stores, some discount stores, or, if you have the budget, you could travel the world collecting sand from colourful beaches) to make the illustration more vibrant.

So even if you can't draw your way out of a paper bag, with a little creativity you can bring your stories to life. I can't draw much more than stick figures (and even that, poorly), but I was able to use my lack of talent to my advantage to create these simple comics.

If I can do it, you can do it.

5 Silly Questions
with Mélanie Watt

JS: Congratulations on winning the Blue Spruce Award for *Scaredy Squirrel*! But I'm concerned: how do you think Scaredy would feel that the award is named after a tree with dangerously sharp needles, as opposed to his safe (and non-pointy) nut tree?

MW: Thank you! Funny you should mention this; when I first informed Scaredy Squirrel that he had won the Blue Spruce Award, he seemed terrified! For a minute there, he thought that this meant that he had actually won a blue spruce tree and needed to move out of his nut tree. I quickly reassured him that this was just the name of the award and that he didn't have to relocate anywhere.

JS: In the beginning of *Scaredy Squirrel Makes a Friend*, there is a warning that everyone must brush their teeth with germ-fighting toothpaste before reading the book. But Scaredy's new friend, the dog, can't brush his teeth, due to a lack of opposable thumbs and a shocking disregard for personal hygiene. Is there any chance that Scaredy will make an exception for him?

MW: In *Scaredy Squirrel Makes a Friend*, Scaredy learns an important lesson: that being yourself is what's important in the end. Sure there will be little inconveniences from time to time, like a wet doggy smell, drool and germs, but that's part of Buddy, and Scaredy loves him the way he is. Especially with a pine-scented air freshener attached to his collar!

This being said, Scaredy still insists that everyone do their personal best to assure good personal hygiene!

JS: Here's a quick timeline I whipped up: August 1, 2006, your penguin book, *Augustine*, is published. November 17, 2006, the penguin movie, *Happy Feet*, is released. June 8, 2007, another penguin movie, *Surf's Up*, is released. The evidence is clear: your books influence the "Next Big Trend" in Hollywood. Do you think a slew of squirrel movies are headed to the big screen, or perhaps a Broadway musical?

MW: Yes, but I hope that the next big trend features Scaredy Squirrel himself!!

JS: Chameleons have the unique ability to change their colour to match their environment. But *Leon the Chameleon* always turns the opposite colour: on a green leaf he turns red, on yellow sand he turns purple and in a blue pond he turns orange. What would happen if Leon tried on Joseph's amazing Technicolor dreamcoat?

MW: He would probably end up on YouTube.

JS: Puisque vous êtes bilingue, vos livres sont disponibles dans les deux langues officielles de notre nation. N'incluez-vous pas des "bouts bonus" dans les versions françaises, que les lecteurs anglais ne pourraient pas comprendre? (Ne vous inquiétez pas, je ne traduirai pas votre réponse.)

MW: Non, au contraire, c'est parfois plus facile d'inclure de l'humour en anglais qu'en français, car il y a plusieurs jeux de mots avec noix en anglais comme: *nutty, in a nut shell,* que je ne peux pas traduire en français.

Mélanie Watt lives in Montreal, Quebec, where she is writing more books about both Scaredy Squirrel and Chester the cat. Her hope for the next big trend featuring Scaredy himself is beginning to come to fruition: a Scaredy television program is currently under development. Mélanie is afraid of sharks, germs and green Martians.

Write Like a Heartthrob

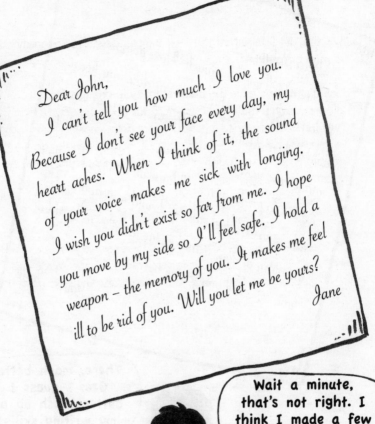

Dear John,
I can't tell you how much I love you, because
I don't. See, your face – every day, my heart
aches when I think of it. The sound of your voice
makes me sick. With longing, I wish you didn't
exist. So far from me, I hope you move. By my
side – so I'll feel safe – I hold a weapon. The
memory of you, it makes me feel ill. To be rid of
you . . . will you let me be?
Yours, Jane
There, much better! Gee, I guess I better brush up on my writing skills.

This section is for all you romantics out there. It will wobble your knees and flutter your hearts. Before we discuss things to consider when writing your love stories, I'm going to call a little black shovel-looking thingee, a little black shovel-looking thingee.

> Oi! I'm a spade!

Boys typically don't like romance. Wait, let me rephrase that. Boys typically won't *admit* they like romance. But love is such an intrinsic part of life that it inevitably becomes a part of almost every book, show and movie. Yes, even the macho action ones! Where would Spider-Man be without Mary Jane? Han Solo without Princess Leia? That ten-foot tall blue avatar without that nine-foot tall blue Na'vi? James Bond without his abundance of love interests?

Anyway, what I'm trying to say is, guys, don't be afraid to add a little romance to your stories. Not only will it make your fiction more well rounded and appealing to a wider audience, but girls love a guy with a sensitive side!

Which brings me to point number one:

1. Romance readers generally prefer a hero with a sensitive side. Perhaps your hero is into classical music, is a vegetarian vampire or isn't afraid to write stories with a little romance in them! Just like you, right? *Right?*

   Alternatively, you could make your hero a bad boy. Perhaps he detests classical music, or is a vampire who drinks the red stuff like it's going out of style. Maybe he's a self-centred jerk who laughs at guys who write stories with a little romance in them. Then have this bad boy romantically change for the sake of the good girl — do it, quick! I'm starting to really hate this guy!

2. Heroines should preferably be intelligent, independent and not too obsessed with love. In fact, you could add a lot of tension to your story if the heroine is initially against the idea of love altogether, but despite her best efforts not to, she gradually begins to fall for the hero.

   Or, maybe your heroine is in search of a boyfriend but unlucky in love. Maybe she's tried dating everyone from the studly star of the basketball team to the geeky dweeb in the mascot outfit, but nothing has worked out for her. Hey, here's an idea! Have her meet the bad boy jerk, initially hate him and then start to fall for him. He'll play it cool but slowly start to fall for her, too. Of course, he'll have to change his ways. It'll be a match made in heaven!

3. Feel free to mix romance with any other genre. Not only does romance work with action and adventure, but it also fits in perfectly with fantasy, science fiction, horror, historical fiction, comedy . . . Like a side of fries or the colour black, love goes with just about everything!

4. Build tension between your couple by keeping them apart. Maybe one hates the other's guts, or they're forced to enrol in different schools, or a pesky love triangle develops. Whatever you decide, it's much more fulfilling if your couple doesn't finally come together until the end of the novel, as opposed to meeting, falling in love and promising themselves to each other all in the first few pages. A good story needs some sort of conflict!

5. Love stories are told to us right from the cradle: fairy tales of brave knights and periled princesses. But what would happen if the gender roles were reversed? What if the knights weren't so brave, and the princesses weren't so perilled? Be bold and turn the classic fairy tale genre on its head!

6. Write from the heart, the gut, the wobbly knees and the light-headed brain. Heck, write from the kidney, liver

and spleen, too. Love is a powerful emotion, so don't be afraid to write with passion. Even Albert Einstein understood the power of romance, as he once said, "Put your hand on a hot stove for a minute, and it seems like an hour. Sit with a pretty girl for an hour, and it seems like a minute. That's relativity."

Remember, all you need is love, and the following books will give you your fair share:

- *Ella Enchanted*, by Gail Carson Levine
- *Philip Hall Likes Me. I Reckon Maybe*, by Bette Greene
- *Deep Down Popular*, by Phoebe Stone
- *Flipped*, by Wendelin Van Draanen

5 Silly Questions
with Loris Lesynski

JS: Not only do you write your own books, but you do your own illustrations as well! You're clearly a very talented multi-tasker; are you also your own editor, bookbinder and distributor?

LL: When I was a kid, I loved playing with printing kits, setting up little rubber letters in wooden racks, so yes, I kind of wish I could print the books myself . . . make the paper . . . even take a pottery class to produce the mugs for my coffee breaks.

I just like *making* things, especially making kids laugh. And enjoy books. But one person can't do everything, especially when they best like spending their time lying around reading. Michael Martchenko is illustrating the books I'm writing these days, which gives me 1. great-looking funny books and 2. lots of lazy reading time, so I'm enormously happy about that.

Actually, lots of other people go into editing, binding and publishing a book, I'm just lucky enough to get my name on it. But I thank all of those other people all the time!

JS: I love *Nothing Beats a Pizza*, but are you sure I'm not going to look like an idiot if I use "pizza" in an intense game of Paper, Rock, Scissors? And what if my opponent uses "dynamite?"

LL: You are such a boy! I didn't mean "beats" in the "beats up" sense, but in the "as good as" sense. Boys are so competitive. If you're starving and it's lunchtime and someone offers you hot, juicy, delicious pizza — enough for both you AND your opponents — that will take your mind off questions involving dynamite, rocks and other weapons. Pizza would make a terrible weapon. Unless it was still frozen, then it could be somewhat useful. That would make a good story, if any of you feel in a writing mood.

JS: One of my favourite books is *Zigzag: Zoems for Zindergarten,* but I just got off the phone with the letter K and he wants to know what your beef is with him.

LL: Clearly, your conversation with K came close to causing a considerable commotion.

K is chronically cranky that his wonderful k-k-k-k sound is often created by the letter C.

But his crummy complaint about my caring attention towards Z is just confusion. I love the K sound! He's the coolest! Why, he's been voted the funniest letter in the alphabet!

Actually, I like all the sounds of all the letters and just about every combo — *brrrrrring, flump, grouse, zubble.* Ahh, poem-writers just *love* words, we do, we do, we do!

JS: When I looked closely at one of the illustrations in *Night School,* I noticed that there are night-friendly books on the classroom's shelf, such as *Goodnight Moon* by Margaret Wise Brown, *Silent Night* by Linda Granfield and . . . *Night School* by Loris Lesynski! The implications of that made my head hurt so much that I forgot what my question about this book was.

LL: Wait a minute, you mean the book that you were reading — *Night School,* by me, Loris Lesynski, was the name of the book on the witchy teacher's desk IN the picture IN the book?

Which means that if Eddie, the "night owl" kid in the story, opened that book on the desk to that page, he would see the book that he was in, which was the book you were reading and holding in your hand?

Which makes me wonder if someone is reading a book about YOU right this minute, and we're just illustrations . . . nah, that couldn't be, because I need a sandwich and a cup of tea and I just drew them and they taste like paper and magic marker, so I must be real . . . but you, I don't know about that.

JS: Can you give us readers a poetic blurb for your poetic book, *"I Did It Because . . ." How a Poem Happens?* (Bonus points if you can work in Ajax, the town where I work!)

LL: I don't know why I write them,
all those stories, all those lines.
I don't know why my head is full of poems
all the time.
"What made you want to be one?"
ask the children when I state
that I longed to be an author from the time
that I was eight.
"The ideas for the book about the ogres,
or *Boy Soup,*
how'd you think them up?" the children ask me
as a group.
"Why'd you change the porridge into pizza
with the bears?"
"Why'd you have the witch throw custard tarts
into the air?"
"Where'd you get the notion for a girl
who turns to stone?"
"Did you write *The Bad Mood Blues* with others
or alone?"
I don't have any answers so I always start
to say,
"I did it just because . . ." and then I shrug
and turn away.
My latest book got named that way,
now you in Ajax know.
Go write a poem of your own. I really mean it —
go!

Loris Lesynski is the creator of eleven (so far!) books for young readers: six storybooks such as Boy Soup, *the rest collections of poems such as* Dirty Dog Boogie *and* I Did It Because . . . *She lives in Toronto and is working on a book of poems making fun of math.*

Don't Forget to Read (Duh!)

Contact Your Favourite Authors . . .
And Ask Them 5 Silly Questions!

Authors spend a lot of their time working alone, imagining far away times and places. So they love it when fans write to them to say they're, well, fans!

Their contact information is often easily found on the Internet. Check their websites for a "contact" page. But if you can't find a way to contact them directly, send them a letter in care of the publishing company that released their most recent book. Most publishers will pass the mail on. If you'd like to get a reply, include a SASE, which is not a sassy gift, but rather, a Self-Addressed Stamped Envelope — an envelope that's addressed to you and already has a stamp. Nothing shows someone you care quite like a SASE.

Once you know where to send your letter, why not send the author five of your very own silly questions?

What's that? You'd like some advice on how to write a silly interview? Well, I could share some of my infinite wisdom on the topic, but then I'd have to kill you . . .

Nah, I'm only kidding. I always wanted to say that.

Anyway, on to my infinite wisdom!

5 Silly Steps to Write an Interview of 5 Silly Questions

1. Pick a silly interviewee. This could be your favourite author, your second favourite author, your third favourite author, your fourth . . . you get the idea. If you decide, however, to interview your least favourite author, *always be respectful.* Although he/she might be #173 on your list of 173, he/she might be number one on someone else's list. And with any luck, you too might be someone's least favourite author one day!

2. Don't limit yourself to authors who write books with silly words in the titles, like "underwear," "farting" or "vice-principal." Just because some authors write serious books doesn't mean they don't have a silly bone in their body. Did you see how silly Robert Munsch was? Wait, that's not a very good example — he's known for his silliness. Let me try that again. Did you see how silly Barbara Haworth-Attard was? Yes, much better example.

3. Don't only read the author's books, but read every interview and article about them that you can find. To prove how important this is I've invented an author: Hoarius McSore. Without knowing anything about Hoarius, the silliest question I can think of for him is, "Did your friends ever call you "Boriest McBore?" However, if I read Hoarius' website and learned that he used to be a high school teacher, I can now ask him, "Did your students ever call you "Boriest McBore?" See? At least three times more silly!

4. Knowing everything about your silly interviewee, put yourself in the silliest frame of mind possible to write the questions. You could read a bunch of silly jokes. You could engage the silliest person you know in conversation for 10 minutes. For me, I sit and stare at a blank wall as I try not to think of anything, mentally flushing my mind like a toilet, then write whatever

questions come to mind first. I've said it before and I'll say it again: clearing my mind comes real easy to me. It's a blessing and a curse.

5. Don't use invisible ink. Or invisible lead. Or an invisible computer. Come to think of it, avoid invisibility all together.

5 Silly Questions
with Joel A. Sutherland

JS: Since I know you get asked this all the time (it helps that we share mind, body and soul), what does your middle initial stand for?

JS: Apples.

JS: Um, okay. I'm relatively sure that's not true, but let's move on. Why bother including the A at all? What would be wrong with simply being credited as Joel Sutherland?

JS: Because apples are my favourite fruit, and I think it's quite uncanny that my favourite fruit is also my middle name, so I want to honour that coincidence on the covers of my books without calling myself Joel Apples Sutherland, because if I did, whatever small shred of credibility and/or respect and/or worship I may attain would be jeopardized. Plus, I don't want to alienate the banana-loving readers of the world. Good enough for you?

JS: Geez, this whole middle name thing is quite the thorn in your side, isn't it?

JS: Is that seriously your question? It has absolutely nothing to do with my writing or with me as a writer. It's an even more useless question than the one you asked Jeremy Tankard about what he points his furniture at. Here's a question for you, Mr. Silly Question Man: are you a graduate of the Silly School for Silly Simpletons?

JS: Well, no, I actually graduated from some fairly respectable schools, and I don't think the Silly School for Silly Simpletons actually exists, and . . . wait a minute, I'm asking the questions here, not you! Fine, I'll drop the middle name thing and ask a question about this book. Do you think it's slightly preposterous for an interviewer and an interviewee to be the same person?

JS: Absolutely, or my name isn't Joel Apples Sutherland!

JS: Oh, come on! There's no way your middle name is Apples, and I should know! Just tell us what the A really stands for!

Note: This interview could not be completed, as the interviewee got up and walked out on the interviewer. It is believed he went outside and ate a pear.

Afterword

Final Tip 1
If you can't cram everything you wanted to say into your book, never fear — just add an afterword!

I don't actually have anything else to say. This might be a first for me. . .

Well, I suppose now that I've got your attention I should put *something* here, so I'll give the final word to someone far wiser than me:

I find television very educational. Every time someone switches it on I go into another room and read a good book.
~Groucho Marx

About the Author

Final Tip 2

People are nosy by nature, so you should write a little bit about yourself to include at the back of the book — if you write in the third person, it'll sound more sophisticated. Also, include a photograph, preferably one that makes you look sophisticated. Author bios are really all about making you appear more sophisticated than you are in real life. I thought I'd get creative and include a photo of me that also tells you a little bit about what makes me tick:

Joel A. Sutherland makes his living as a librarian, and is surrounded by books both at work and at home. His first adult novel, *Frozen Blood*, was nominated for the Bram Stoker Award in 2009. Among his favourite foods are apples and grilled cheese sandwiches (pictured). Joel lives in Courtice, Ontario, with his wife, Colleen (who was ironically teased as a girl for being destined to marry a librarian), their son, future librarian Charles, and their one-hundred-pound Goldendoodle, Murphy. Despite their dog's size, they've still made room in their house for a mountain of books.

Looking for even more words of wisdom? Check out these other great books about creative writing:

- *Once Upon a Time: Creative Writing Fun for Kids*, by Annie Buckley and Kathleen Coyle
- *Kids Write! Fantasy & Sci Fi, Mystery, Autobiography, Adventure & More!* by Rebecca Olien
- *Writing Magic: Creating Stories that Fly*, by Gail Carson Levine
- *Extraordinary Short Story Writing*, by Steven Otfinoski
- *How Writers Work: Finding a Process that Works for You*, by Ralph Fletcher
- *Meet Canadian Authors & Illustrators*, by Alison Gertridge